Library and Information Centres
Red Doles Lane
Huddersfield, West Yorkshire
HD2 1YF

KT-471-068

This book should be returned on
Fines are charged if the item is la

Praise for

...onships with...
...ost, poetic prose and fee...
THE ...

*There are so many great things that ... about this book ...
a very original debut read and on... to be missed. This is
a book that should be read and will be loved by many ...*
MR RIPLEY'S ENCHANTED BOOKS blog

Highly original without being overtly quirky.
GLASGOW HERALD

*This magical and enlightening adventure story, set against the atmospheric
backdrop of the Scottish coast, is a touching tale of friendship and
hidden strengths ... an extraordinary, must-read story.*
LANCASHIRE EVENING POST

*Another brilliant book from Chicken House. This is Enid Blyton and Malcolm
Saville for the 21st century's young readers. I can't fault it, it took me back to
my own teenage years when I was desperate for adventure stories like this.*
BOOKS MONTHLY

A haunting, evocative tale ...
CBI RECOMMENDED READS

*A suspenseful novel, full of secrets and betrayals, this book is a real page turner ...
The plot is gripping from page one and rolls on in the most compelling manner
from there ... [a] very satisfying read with wide appeal and enduring charm.*
SCHOOL LIBRARIAN JOURNAL

*... the novel's mysterious air and substantive plotlines involving divorce, human
trafficking, and the challenges of adolescence will keep readers hooked.*
BOOKLIST (USA)

800667489

A MESSAGE FROM CHICKEN HOUSE

I love the wilds of Scotland's Highlands and Islands. At dusk, or in the gloaming, I often hear the most mysterious sounds. But *nothing* prepared me for the ghostly howl of the long-lost wolves in this brilliantly exciting story. Kerr's novel will immerse you in the wilding of nature, the strength of an ancient mystery and the lure of an impossible challenge. *The Rise of Wolves* is more than a fantastic thriller – it's a call to protect everything we love!

BARRY CUNNINGHAM
Publisher
Chicken House

The Rise of Wolves

Kerr Thomson

2 Palmer Street, Frome,
Somerset BA11 1DS

Text © Kerr Thomson 2017
Cover illustration © Frances Castle 2017

First published in Great Britain in 2017
Chicken House
2 Palmer Street
Frome, Somerset BA11 1DS
United Kingdom
www.chickenhousebooks.com

Kerr Thomson has asserted his right under the Copyright, Designs and
Patents Act 1988 to be identified as the author of this work.

All rights reserved.
No part of this publication may be reproduced or transmitted or utilized
in any form or by any means, electronic, mechanical, photocopying
or otherwise, without the prior permission of the publisher.

Cover and interior design by Steve Wells
Typeset by Dorchester Typesetting Group Ltd
Printed and bound in Great Britain by CPI Group (UK) Ltd, Croydon, CR0 4YY

The paper used in this Chicken House book is made
from wood grown in sustainable forests.

1 3 5 7 9 10 8 6 4 2

British Library Cataloguing in Publication data available.

PB ISBN 978-1-911077-69-5
eISBN 978-1-911077-99-2

For Samuel

Chapter 1

The howl pierced the darkening sky and made Innis Munro stop dead in his tracks. He pulled his hood down, listened intently. The only sound was his beating heart.

That was a wolf, he thought.

But it couldn't have been. There were no wolves on the island of Nin, no wolves in Scotland any more, not for almost three hundred years. It was just a trick of the wind.

He pressed on but kept his hood down. The afternoon light of early March was fading fast, snow was falling, and he was still a good half-mile from home.

Innis walked faster, told himself it was not the howl that made him hurry but the gloomy sky and gathering snow. He was crossing 'the Barrens' – the middle of the island where the land was hummocky and boggy.

At the northern edge of the moorland stood a mountain called *Beinn Ainmhidhean*. Translated from Gaelic, it was the Hill of the Beasts, and Innis went there to watch the golden eagles that nested on its crags. The mountain was the only feature on the landscape. A few stumpy birch trees clung to the hollows but this was empty land; no crofts, no roads, no people.

To a stranger, a mainlander, it would have seemed he was lost in the middle of bleak nowhere, but Innis knew this ground, knew every rise and dip, every boggy pool and gorse bush. His grandfather's croft was over the next ridge and he knew Gramps would have the peat fire roaring and something thick and tasty simmering in a pot.

Another howl came; long, bloodcurdling, wolf-like.

Innis stopped again, caught his breath and held it. He turned full circle, scanning the landscape, peering through the snow and the gloom. Closer this time.

It was someone playing a trick, trying to frighten him. Someone from school looking to mock him in a new and different way. It was pretty lame, actually. There were no wolves on Nin.

Innis cupped a hand to his mouth and returned the best horror-movie wolf howl he could muster. There was an immediate response but from further away this time, in the distance up by the mountain. And then another howl, much closer, a sound that no boy could make.

Innis whirled around and stared across the moor. Twenty paces from where he stood was a shape, dark against the brightness of swirling snow. The silhouette of an animal. It stood side-on to him, front and back legs splayed, back arched, bushy tail curved down. Innis watched the creature raise its head slowly to the sky and another howl shattered the silence.

It was the unmistakable silhouette of a wolf.

Innis turned and ran, leaping across the marshy ground, rasping air in and out. He slid down shallow slopes and sank into boggy puddles, rammed hands into the mud to haul himself out, moved forwards at speed, too frightened to look back in case the wolf was upon him and his legs gave out. In the distance, he saw the lights of four crofts that sat nestled below the higher ground of the Barrens. Home. He took a glance behind as he ran, saw nothing and stumbled and fell, landing face first in the marsh.

Innis sat up, felt water ooze beneath his trousers and melting snow run down his back. He gave a shiver and looked around. No wolves – but a boy was walking towards him, the snow lying thick enough now to hear the crunch of his steps.

Innis struggled to his feet. He didn't recognize the boy.

'Are you okay?' asked a gruff voice.

'I'm fine, I just tripped.'

The boy hesitated for a moment, then said, 'All right then.'

He was smaller than Innis but seemed older, maybe fourteen or fifteen. In appearance, the boys were the exact opposite. Innis was tall and thin with lanky legs and straggly black hair. The stranger was squat, with short, fair hair, shaved almost to the scalp. He had dark, unfriendly eyes. Innis didn't know him.

The boy turned and took a step away, and Innis asked, 'Where are you going?'

'What's it to you?' the boy asked, without turning or stopping.

He was heading inland, across the Barrens. 'There's a wolf out there,' Innis said.

The boy stopped and headed back towards Innis. 'Where exactly?'

Innis pointed. 'Out there somewhere.'

'You saw it?' probed the boy.

'I heard it *and* I saw it.'

The boy didn't answer, asked instead, 'How far?'

'Not far, five minutes from here.'

The boy sighed and wiped snow from his face. He turned and strode off without another word.

Chapter 2

I nnis shivered as he slid down the slope from the higher land of the moor and walked along the rough track that led towards the crofts; four small, low cottages with whitewashed walls of thick stone and chimneys that spouted smoke. They sat alone on the edge of the Barrens, two hundred metres inland from the cliffs of Nin's eastern coast. The crofts lay a mile or so north of Skulavaig, the island's only town.

His house was fourth in line and as he passed the first he saw a girl in the back garden, big flakes of snow falling around her. Katrina McColl, neighbour and school friend. His only neighbour really. His only friend. She was thirteen like him, but where he had black hair, she had long brown hair, the same colour as her eyes. She was average height – smaller than Innis – and had a very pretty face, which he had only recently noticed. She was dismantling a large telescope.

Innis pushed through a small gate in a low wall, into her garden.

'Hi Kat,' he said. She was the easiest person in the world to talk to. Kat got him.

The girl turned and laughed. 'What happened to you?'

'I fell.'

'Were you skiing?'

'I was running.' He was about to explain why but she spoke before he could.

'Help me with this telescope.'

'Why are you taking it apart? You've got a waterproof cover.'

'I'm worried snow might build up overnight. The tripod could snap with the weight.'

Innis held the telescope steady while the girl carefully unscrewed each part. It was a Newtonian reflector telescope with a 200mm mirror that could observe far-flung star clusters as well as the moon up close. It had cost her over £300 and had been her last birthday, Christmas and six months' pocket money put together.

He helped her carry the telescope tube and its heavy mount into a small brick shed at the bottom of the garden. 'You wouldn't have seen much tonight anyway.'

'I know, it's such a shame. I was going to find the rings of Saturn.'

Innis took a breath and said, 'Do you know what I saw earlier?'

'What?'

'Out on the Barrens.'

'What?'

'It's why I was running, why I fell.'

'What?!' she said, exasperated.

Innis took another breath. 'A wolf.'

Kat laughed and gave him a look of disbelief.

'I did, straight up. Did you not hear it howl?'

'No, I did not hear a wolf howl. There are no wolves on Nin. Years and years ago, aye, not any more.'

'I know what I saw.'

'You saw a big dog, if you saw anything.'

'Dogs don't howl.'

'Of course they do.'

'Not like that. Not like a wolf.'

Kat gave her best wolf howl and punched him on the arm.

From the kitchen window of the croft a woman's voice said, 'Katrina, you'll wake the baby.'

'Sorry, Mum.'

'Is that you, Innis?' asked the voice.

'Aye, it is.'

'How's your grandfather?'

'He's fine.' Innis's tone was positive, but Kat was watching and he knew his eyes said something different.

'Tell Katrina to put away that contraption and get in

where it's warm.'

'She never calls it a telescope,' the girl said. 'It's always *that contraption*.'

'Did you see the boy up on the moor?' Innis asked.

'What boy?'

'He went off to look for the wolf.'

She laughed again. 'Did you bang your head when you fell?'

Innis sighed. When said out loud, his story seemed unlikely. 'I'm going home.'

'What are you doing tomorrow?'

'Nothing much. You'll be at church.'

'After church. Do you want to build a snowman?'

He moved back down the path towards the gate. 'Isn't that a song?'

'A snowball fight, at least.'

'The snow will have melted.'

'If it hasn't.'

'Then we'll do every snow-filled activity we can think of.'

He heard her say, *whoopee*, as the gate closed behind him. It rarely snowed in the Western Isles of Scotland. The surrounding ocean kept the temperature a little warmer than the mainland. When it did snow, it never lasted long.

Innis walked down the track towards his own croft. There was no wall around his house. It was small and low with chimneys at both ends and narrow windows that didn't let in much light by day, but gave a welcoming glow in the dark. Instead of opening the front door, he moved around to the back of the building for a last look out over the Barrens. The falling snow was lighter now and the land was lit by its whiteness, so he could see quite far across the rumpled ground and make out the peak of the mountain in the distance. There was no sign of movement except snow flurrying in the breeze. He cocked an ear and listened, held his breath, but the snow brought a quiet to the air, a muffling of sound that silenced even the wind. He listened again, but the wolves no longer howled.

Chapter 3

The morning sun was streaming through the windows as Innis shuffled from his bedroom into the warm kitchen, where his grandfather was having difficulty cutting up the eggy bread he had made for breakfast.

'I'll get that, Gramps.'

His grandfather waved him away. 'Sit yourself down. You've a ferry to catch.'

'It's Sunday. No school today.'

Gramps paused as he reached for two large mugs of steaming tea, his eyes tightening. 'Aye, Sunday, of course it is.'

'How's the snow?'

'Mostly melted. It never lies on Nin.'

Innis gave a groan of disappointment. 'Kat and I were

going to build a snowman.'

'I cannae remember the last time I saw one of them. There was one winter when it snowed like never before. I was just a lad and me and Davey, that's old Davey, we did all those things and got frostnip in our fingers because we wouldnae wear gloves.' Gramps gave a chuckle and returned to the stove.

Old Davey was Katrina McColl's grandfather and he and Gramps were cousins. Which meant that Innis and Kat were related, they were *third* cousins. Innis sat at a small table close by the fire and cupped his tea and stared into the blaze. He was still half asleep and couldn't get warm. It was as if the snow had seeped under his skin.

'Where's your mother?' his grandfather asked. 'Her breakfast will get cold.'

Innis sighed as he watched the old man shakily place another plate on the table. Gramps could remember getting frostbite in his fingers seventy years earlier, but had forgotten that his mum had already returned to the mainland, where she managed a hotel. She came home for a few days every fortnight but she was in denial about his grandfather's health.

'Mum left yesterday, Gramps.'

The health visitor had stressed to Innis never to say, *have you forgotten?* or *don't you remember?* The lapses in memory were new, the tremors were old and getting worse. His grandfather had Parkinson's disease.

'Aye of course, I know that.'

Innis watched his grandfather stare at the extra plate. The boy reached across and grabbed it. 'Which means more eggy bread for me. I'm starving.'

He *was* hungry – running for your life from shadowy wolves worked up an appetite.

'I've been thinking,' Gramps said. 'Your tale from last night might not be as fanciful as you think.'

This he remembers, Innis thought. 'How do you mean?'

'You said you saw a wolf.'

'It was probably a big dog.'

'Maybe not. There's a place on the north-west of the island, in its far corner. There's only a rough road up to it. It's a kind of wildlife sanctuary.'

'I've never heard of it.'

'Aye, it's all a bit low-key, hush-hush. Run by an old fellow by the name of . . . His name is . . .' The name was gone. 'Anyway, he's the only one out there. I see him in town now and then.'

'What kind of wildlife sanctuary?'

'I thought it was mainly wildcats, red squirrels, that kind of thing. Scottish animals that are under threat. He has some kind of breeding programme going. I wandered by a couple of times but not for a good few years now. He disnae like visitors.'

'And you think he keeps wolves as well?'

'It's unlikely, but I suppose it is a possibility.'

Innis took a mouthful of eggy bread – maybe he

wasn't going mad after all. But if there *were* wolves on Nin, what were they doing roaming the Barrens?

There was silence for a few moments while Innis chewed. From the corner of his eye he could see the twist of his grandfather's mouth as tried to retrieve some information.

'What about your father?' the old man asked eventually. It was a vague question, one of the ways his grandfather tried to mask his forgetfulness.

'Last we spoke he said it was hot and humid in the Gulf of Thailand. Won't be home till summer.'

Innis's father worked in the oil industry, and spent most of the year working on rigs abroad. Innis suspected he could get home more often if he wanted to, but his father wasn't island-born and often gave the impression that Nin was as much a foreign land as the places he had worked in Asia and Africa.

Innis saw his grandfather nod, a memory sparked. Most of the time it was just him and Gramps, and that was how he liked it. But he wondered how long it would be before things became too difficult, before they wouldn't allow it any more.

Innis spent the morning waiting for Kat to come home. The girl attended Sunday worship every week, wore a small silver cross around her neck and declared herself a Christian. Her church was up by the lighthouse. Gramps was a member there as well but he rarely attended, even less so in recent months. Innis had been a few times but only to keep his grandfather company.

There was enough sunshine in the second week of March for the snow to have mostly melted. It lingered only at the bottom of the hollows on the moorland. The air was cold, producing puffs of breath as Innis stood at the edge of the Barrens. He had wanted to look for wolf prints this morning but the snow had disappeared. The memory of the wolf howl seemed to be melting away as well. Had he imagined it? He looked to the sky – brilliant blue without a single cloud. There would be no more snow today. Perhaps no more this year, now that spring had officially begun.

The sound of a car coming down the track made him head towards Kat's croft, scraping together a handful of snow as he went. An old, battered Land Rover pulled up and the McColl family piled out; first the two older brothers, who gave Innis a body swerve, then Kat's mum with the baby and her dad, who nodded hello, and then finally Kat herself, clutching a black leather bible that curled at the corners.

Innis tossed the snowball in her direction. Kat must have been expecting it because she instantly raised her bible as a shield and the snow crumbled against it.

'I told you Jesus saves,' she said with a smile.

'I don't think we'll manage a snowman. Fancy a bike ride instead?'

'Where to?'

'The other side of the island.'

'What for?'

He paused, then said boldly, 'We're going on a wolf hunt.'

Chapter 4

Innis and Kat cycled side by side along the thin stretch of tarmac that curved around the north of the island. Innis had explained where they were going and why, even though Kat hadn't asked. They wore hats and gloves and rode fast to keep warm in the frigid air. The road was quiet; they had met only two cars, both heading in the opposite direction. There wasn't much up in this part of the island; a few crofts, a church that was empty now that morning service was finished and a lighthouse that was even emptier, the lighthouse keepers replaced by machines.

As he cycled, Innis constantly scanned the moorland to his left, expecting the sleek shape of a running wolf to appear over every ridge. All he saw were rabbits and, in the distance, red deer. The road began to curve to the south and move away from the coast, around the bottom of a wide inlet called Loch Nin. There was a point of land west of the inlet that his grandfather had said was the location of the wildlife sanctuary.

He cycled past a rough track that wound north and pulled hard on his brakes, Kat skidding to a stop beside him.

'What is it?' she asked.

'I think this is it,' he said, pointing to the track, which was no more than a thin rut. 'Gramps said it's hard to get to by road.'

'Are you sure there's something up here?'

'Not really.' Innis pushed down on the pedals and turned his bike on to the track. 'Only one way to find out.'

They cycled slowly up the trail, a cold wind picking up as they drew closer to the sea. The path rose upwards so that all they could see ahead was blue sky. The land was still and quiet, the only sound the faraway honk of a greylag goose from somewhere over the moorland. The track levelled out and a closed gate barred the way. A sign read, PRIVATE PROPERTY. NO ENTRY.

'Oh dear,' Kat said with a mischievous smile, 'We'll have to turn back.'

'You only hang a sign like that if you have something to hide,' Innis said.

'Like a pack of wolves.'

'Exactly.'

'Or a pride of lions.'

'Probably not.'

'Or a herd of woolly mammoths.'

'Too far.'

The girl smiled and a twinkle lit her eyes. 'Let's go and see.'

She pushed her bike on to the moorland and around the gate, then remounted and pedalled on. Innis followed. They cycled for a minute more and then the track dipped down and there was the ocean sparkling in the bright sun, the island of Skye beyond, filling the horizon. Perched close to the clifftop was a group of buildings. A wisp of smoke curled from the chimney of a small croft to the side.

'Someone lives here,' Innis said.

They cycled closer, down the track, and saw that the buildings had various cages and enclosures attached. Dogs began to bark and they both pulled on their brakes and stopped at the corner of a tall wire fence that stretched away over the moorland. Innis peered inside but couldn't see anything. The place smelt like a zoo and he had the eerie sense of a thousand eyes watching him.

'What are you doing here?' shouted a stern voice from behind them.

Innis and Kat whirled around. A man stood there with a scowl on his face and a shotgun in the crook of his arm. He was short but stocky, with a mass of unruly greying hair and an unshaven chin. He wore stained dungarees and wellies.

'This is private property,' he said. 'You cannae be on this land. Be off with you.'

Innis looked at the man and then his gun and then the man again. This had been a stupid idea.

Kat was not to be intimidated. 'I hope that thing isn't loaded,' she said. 'It's dangerous to wave a loaded gun at two children out on a bike ride.'

'What do you want?' the man asked.

'We're just exploring,' said the girl.

'Well, there's nothing to see here.'

Kat waved her arms towards the pens and cages. 'What's all this then?'

'Do as my uncle says,' cried another voice, and Innis and Kat turned to see a figure emerge from a small building further down the track.

'You,' Innis said.

It was the boy from the night before. In spite of the cold, he was wearing only wellies, shorts and a T-shirt.

'Get away from here,' the boy said, 'while you still have air in your tyres.'

The man said, 'It's fine Lachlan, our young explorers were just leaving.'

Innis looked at the boy called Lachlan. There was an unblinking iciness to his eyes and a mouth set in a menacing sneer. They were clearly not to be made welcome, not to get the tour, not to have their queries answered. But there was one thing Innis had to know, the reason he had cycled all this way on a frosty day. He was going to ask his question.

'Where are the wolves?'

The scruffy man and the surly boy looked at each other in alarm and Innis knew for certain that there *had* been a wolf on Nin.

'I dinnae ken what you're talking about, laddie.'

'I saw one last night, out on the Barrens.'

'There are no wolves here.'

Kat reached over and gave the wire fence beside her a shake. 'What do you keep in here then?'

The man hesitated, then said, 'That's a pen for wildcats.'

'I can't see any wildcats.'

'You willnae see anything if you keep shaking the fence.'

Lachlan laughed.

'Are there wildcats on Nin?' asked Innis.

'Not any longer,' said the man, 'but the plan is to reintroduce them. We have a breeding programme here for genetically pure wildcats. The problem is that they breed with feral domesticated cats. We're one of the last holdouts of the authentic Scottish wildcat. Our work here is very important.'

'Wildcats, not wolves,' Lachlan said coldly.

'So it was wildcats you were chasing on the Barrens last night?' Innis asked.

'That's right.'

'In the snow?'

'That's right. Why were *you* there?'

The boy had a point. 'I was heading home.'

The man spoke again. 'And that sounds like a grand idea right now. The pair of you get back home.'

Innis looked to Kat, but she seemed out of ideas. 'Come on,' he said, wheeling his bike in a circle.

The island of Nin liked its mysteries, its intrigues, its legends and myths. It was an island full of bleak moors and dark caves, ancient castles and hidden lochs. Innis looked back at the cluster of cages and buildings and knew there were secrets here. A new mystery on an island full of old ones.

Chapter 5

Innis cycled until he was out of sight of the wildlife sanctuary then pulled on the brake and jumped off his bike.

'What are you doing?' Kat asked.

'They're hiding something back there.'

'Aye, maybe, but it isn't wolves.'

'Are you not curious?'

'No. It's too cold and I want to get home.'

'I'm going for a look.'

'Well, try not to get shot. That man had a gun.'

'He wouldn't do that.'

The girl gave a look with raised eyebrows that said, *how do you know?* and cycled away. Innis half hid his bike under some thick heather and began to walk across the moor in the direction of the wildlife sanctuary. He bent low as he approached the huddle of buildings. They were crowded together, with a stretch of open ground sloping down to the edge of the island. Innis sneaked along the clifftop, hoping he was low enough to be out of sight. The ocean sparkled in the sun far below, and out on the water a small lobster boat made slow progress towards the north.

For all that he was an island boy, Innis had never loved the ocean. It frightened him. He preferred inland, across the Barrens. He liked the quiet there, he liked the sky, he liked the emptiness. He turned his head from the water, shuddering slightly, and something caught his eye further along the cliff edge. The cliff seemed to disappear. He crept along the top and saw that the cliff had a narrow inlet, as if a chunk had slipped into the sea. The gap was deep and the waves made a booming sound at the bottom.

He peered over the edge. It was a long drop to the ocean below. Waves crashed hard against jagged rocks sticking out from the water. It made his stomach turn and he took a step backwards, then another, then a third. His foot tripped on something and he tumbled backwards on to his bottom.

A rock stuck up from the ground. He looked closely and saw it was a shaped stone. The surface was weathered and covered with moss, sand and bird poo, but there was a trace of writing. He rubbed the stone with his gloved hand and words emerged, four of them.

THE BONNIE LADDIE'S LEAP

What is this? he wondered. *Who is the 'Bonnie Laddie'?*

The sound of quick footsteps made him look up. He only had time to see Lachlan bearing down on him before he was sent sprawling on to his back, Lachlan's hand pressing down on his face. Innis's neck bent back and he realized there was nothing beneath his head. He was out beyond the edge of the cliff. Far beneath him waves smacked powerfully against the rock face.

'Get off me!' Innis cried.

'What are you doing?' Lachlan snarled.

'I wasn't doing anything.'

'You shouldn't be here.'

'Let me up!'

The boy pushed harder. Lachlan was shorter than Innis but he had thick arms and a broad chest and was much stronger.

'Please, let me go.'

'This is private property.' Lachlan's face was red with rage and flecks of spittle hung from his lips. 'You've no business coming here and snooping around.'

'Okay, okay, I'm sorry.' Innis felt the boy's grip slacken. 'I'll leave.'

'And never come back.'

'And never come back.'

'You promise?'

'I promise.'

'Otherwise you *will* go for a swim.' Lachlan pushed himself up, grabbed Innis by the front of his jacket and hauled him to his feet. He shoved him roughly.

'Go on, get lost.'

Innis stumbled back along the clifftop, and turned when he thought there was enough distance between him and the boy. 'You're off your head, so you are,' he shouted.

Lachlan stood with fists clenched by his side, breathing heavily.

'And don't you forget it!'

Chapter 6

Monday morning. Innis stood at the back of the ferry and watched the island of Nin shrink and lose its features until it was just a black silhouette on a silver ocean. This was the usual Monday routine, catching the ferry to school. Nin did not have enough children to justify a high school of its own; children from all the small islands in the area attended high school on the big island of Skye. As the journey was too long and the weather often too stormy for daily travel, the pupils stayed Monday night to Thursday night in a purpose-built hostel attached to the school, returning home after lessons on Friday.

Innis always felt strange when leaving the island; desperate to be gone yet missing it already. This contradiction was just one of many that began and ended with his name. Innis Munro. In Gaelic, *Innis* meant island; a *Munro* was a mountain above three thousand feet. Island and mountain, one of the ocean, one of the land. Was he a sailor or a mountaineer? Innis laughed to himself – he didn't like water and he didn't like heights.

'Why are you smiling?' asked Kat as she appeared beside him.

'I didn't know I was.'

'You've got a big cheesy.'

'I think it's a grimace.'

'Monday morning will do that to you.'

Innis scoffed. 'You love school.'

'I love learning. I don't necessarily love school.'

'Aye, well, school loves you.'

'I only do well because I work hard and study for tests. You should try it sometime.'

Innis gave her an unamused smile and rubbed his hands together to warm them up. It was difficult enough concentrating in school without other, more pressing thoughts crowding his brain. He needed to know more about that mysterious corner of his island, with its carved stone and weird family.

A morning of English followed by Science felt long, even though these were his two favourite subjects. Thoughts of wolves kept ruining his focus. At break time, as Innis walked past the History department, he had a sudden idea. Mr Rivans was a History teacher whose white hair and craggy face made him look as if he'd lived through most of the historical periods that featured in the curriculum. The Scottish Wars of Independence, the American Civil War, the First World War; Mr Rivans had fought in them all. Innis liked Mr Rivans. When he entered the classroom, the teacher looked up with a scowl.

'Young Munro, no less,' he said. 'I thought when you left my class last year you wouldnae cross my door again.'

'I need your help,' Innis said.

Mr Rivans snorted. 'You're a bit late laddie, you failed all your tests.'

'I knew the interesting bits. You just asked the wrong questions.'

The teacher gave a bemused sigh. 'That, my boy, is the idler's excuse.' He turned back to his jotters. 'So, what do you want?'

'I found a carved stone with writing on it. It was beside a cliff on my island.'

'And what island is that?'

'Nin.'

Mr Rivans nodded and said, 'Aye, that's right, a Nin boy,' as if that explained everything. 'And what did this writing say?'

'"The Bonnie Laddie's Leap".'

The teacher looked up, a hint of curiosity on his face.

'The Bonnie Laddie's Leap,' he repeated. 'Did you not just google it? That's all everyone does these days.'

'I tried that. Nothing. I even went to the library first thing and looked in some books, but there's nothing.'

'Consulting a book, now there's a notion.' Mr Rivans shook his head. 'I've heard the phrase but I cannae think where. Leave it with me, I suppose, and I'll investigate.'

Innis thanked him and left the classroom, thinking that perhaps he should have tried a little harder in Mr Rivans's class. He quite enjoyed the subject but there were too many dates to remember. Dates were just numbers, and numbers were a serious problem.

Innis suffered from a learning difficulty called dyscalculia. Some people called it number blindness, others called it maths dyslexia. Innis just knew he wasn't any good at sums. His dyscalculia was severe enough to receive learning support in Maths and Science and it held him back in other subjects as well. In Geography he struggled with map grid references, in Home Economics he could never measure out ingredients, in Music he couldn't follow a rhythm, in Art he had difficulty with scale and perspective. Teachers who hadn't checked his school profile thought him stupid or lazy. Teachers who knew about his dyscalculia often assumed it was just in Maths he needed extra help. It was easy to forget that the ability to work with numbers was essential in every aspect of life. Away from school, he could never remember phone numbers, he still sometimes got his left and right mixed up, and he was always losing track of time. In school, he was seen as a listless klutz. But on his island he was none of those things; it was just him and Gramps and Kat and the birds out on the Barrens.

After school, Innis met Kat in the hostel common room. Boys and girls had their own accommodation blocks and the separation was strictly policed. There was also a games room and a TV room, but the common room was always quieter. There was still an hour before dinner and Kat was doing her homework when Innis entered the room.

'Did you see him?' she exclaimed, rising from her chair.

'See who?'

'That boy from yesterday. Lachlan.'

'See him where?'

'In school. He's at school.'

'No.'

'He's in my English class.'

'No.' Innis didn't want it to be true. 'Are you sure?'

'Of course I'm sure. Ms Michie read out his name – Lachlan Geddes. I said hello at the end of class but he ignored me completely.'

'But he looks older.'

'Held back a year, I heard.'

'I never saw him. And he wasn't on the ferry this morning. And where is he now?' Panic gripped Innis. 'Is he staying in the hostel?'

'He's not, I asked.'

'So where is he? He can't have gone back to Nin.'

She shrugged. 'He's a man of mystery.'

'He's not mysterious, he's psycho.'

Kat laughed. 'You never told me what you discovered yesterday.'

Innis remembered looking down at the crashing waves below as he dangled over the edge of the cliff. 'Nothing. There was nothing to see.'

'Are you doing your homework?'

'Later.'

He turned and headed back out, heard Kat say, 'I'll help you if you like.' He didn't want her help tonight, although he probably needed it. Instead, he went to his room and threw himself on his bed. Having wolfboy in the same school would be a nightmare. As if there weren't already enough idiots making his life miserable.

Chapter 7

On the way to registration on Tuesday morning, Innis kept glancing over his shoulder, expecting to see Lachlan Geddes ready to pounce. If not the boy himself then a rabid wolf he kept on a chain. Innis's registration teacher informed him that Mr Rivans would like to see him at morning interval. Periods one and two passed with no sign of Lachlan and when the bell rang, Innis reported to Mr Rivans as instructed.

'I did a wee bit of research,' the History teacher said, shuffling things on his desk. 'It's a fascinating story, your Bonnie Laddie's Leap.'

'So what's it all about?' Innis asked.

Mr Rivans handed him some pages of paper. 'I printed off some notes for you. I always like to see a student take a keen interest in history.'

Innis thought a *keen* interest was stretching it.

'So, tell me, Innis,' Mr Rivans said. 'Who *is* the Bonnie Laddie?'

Innis shrugged. 'I've no idea. That's why I came to you.'

The teacher frowned. 'Seriously, no idea at all?' Innis shook his head and Mr Rivans did likewise with a sigh. 'You've heard of Bonnie Prince Charlie?'

'Aye, of course,' said Innis. 'He wanted to be King of Scotland.'

'Not just Scotland. England and Ireland as well. It was called the Jacobite rising. Do you know when it was?'

Dates. Numbers. Figures. They left Innis floundering. 'A long time ago,' he said.

Mr Rivans laughed. 'That's very true. Charles Edward Stuart, Bonnie Prince Charlie as he's known, came from France to Scotland in 1745 to claim the British throne and was defeated at the famous battle of Culloden only a year later. He fled from the government army, was chased across the Highlands and Islands, and that's where your little mystery comes in.'

'He's the Bonnie Laddie?'

'That he is. Legend says he spent a couple of nights hiding out on your island, Nin. At one point, he was almost caught on a clifftop by a band of soldiers but he leapt across a large gap in the rocks and made his escape.'

Innis remembered the large cleft in the cliff face. 'The Bonnie Laddie's Leap,' he said. It seemed unlikely that someone could jump across the gap, but running for your life would put power in your legs.

'A Nin man called Hamish Geddes took the Prince to the mainland in a small boat, and from there he returned to France.'

'The man's name was Geddes?' Innis asked. That was Lachlan's name.

'Aye, that's right. The leap is just a tale, of course,' Mr Rivans added. 'There's no real evidence that it's true.'

One small mystery cleared up. 'Well, thanks for finding that out,' Innis said.

Mr Rivans gave a sly smile. 'Oh that's only half the story, believe me.' He nodded towards the paper Innis held in his hand. 'But I'll let you read the rest. It's break time and I'm away for a cup of tea.'

Innis left the classroom and headed for the PE department, too late now to join the queue for a muffin. As he passed the door to the stairs he heard a commotion in the stairwell. He peered through the glass of the door and saw the backs of three senior boys. They had formed a tight huddle around someone and were taunting and jeering. Innis was about to turn swiftly and scarper, glad it wasn't him this time, when he caught a glimpse of the target. It was Lachlan Geddes.

The huddle loosened a little as the three older boys took a step back. Innis could see Lachlan's fists clenched, a look of hate on his face. If Lachlan was going down he was taking somebody with him. He was smaller and younger and outnumbered, and for a second Innis admired the boy's bravery. Part of him wanted to see Lachlan get a taste of his own medicine, but he was a Nin boy, and Nin boys looked out for one another. Or so Innis assumed. It had never been tested before.

He pushed open the door to the stairs and said in the most confident voice he could muster, 'Are you Lachlan Geddes?'

The three senior boys turned and gave Innis a collection of menacing looks.

'What do you want, slugface?' asked the biggest of the brutes.

'I've a message from Mr MacDonald,' Innis said. 'He wants to see Lachlan Geddes now and I've to escort him to his office.'

Mr MacDonald was the very scary head teacher. No one was summoned to his office to be told how well they were doing.

'Ooohh,' said the three thugs in unison, anticipating the trouble the new boy must be in.

'Come on,' Innis said to Lachlan, 'Before MacDonald really loses it.'

Lachlan moved past the older boys and got a shove in the back.

'Next time,' said one of them.

Lachlan squared up to his adversary. 'Aye well, next time maybe there will only be the one of you, and then we'll see.'

The three brutes laughed, but Innis could see in their nervous eyes that none of them fancied being alone with the mad new boy.

Innis pulled Lachlan's arm before anything else happened. 'Come on, let's go.'

He pushed through the door, out into the play-ground, where pupils stood in groups chatting or swiping their phones. The bell rang for the end of morning break and the students moved as one towards their classrooms.

Innis turned to Lachlan. 'We'll go a different way.'

'What about the head teacher?'

'There's no message from MacDonald. I just said that to get you away from those idiots.'

Lachlan stopped and was jostled by students moving past him. He had a look of disgusted disbelief on his face. 'You were *saving* me?'

'They're not nice guys, those three.'

'I didn't need saving. I can sort out my own problems.'

'You just looked a bit outnumbered.'

'I'm outnumbered when they bring a shinty team with their sticks. Otherwise I can look after myself.'

'I was just trying to help.'

'Well don't. Stay away from me on Nin and stay away from me here at school. I don't need a friend.'

The boy strode off in the opposite direction and walked out the front gate of the school. *Well that's an* unauthorized absence *right there*, Innis thought. He wished he had let the senior boys have their way.

I don't need a friend.

As if.

He moved towards the gym changing room, already dreading the next fifty minutes of swinging for and completely missing a shuttlecock.

Chapter 8

Tuesday evening found Innis and Kat sitting on a bench in the fading light and cold air, listening to waves roll up a shingle beach.

'I wish you'd tell me why we're here,' Innis said.

Kat was reading by the light of her phone. 'All in good time. We need to wait until it's properly dark.'

'You do realize it's after eight. We're supposed to be in the hostel by eight.'

Kat offered her mischievous smile. 'Who's to know?'

Katrina McColl was the model pupil and perfect daughter; hard-working, well-behaved, super-ambitious, church-going. It seemed to Innis that sometimes this perfection hung like a weight around her neck. Every now and then she would throw it off; a twinkle would light her eyes and a sly smile would curl her lips and she would do something naughty. Nothing bad or evil, just something that broke the rules, an unexpected act of disobedience or minor rebellion. It was like a release, and she was always very careful never to get caught.

She turned off the light and held up the documents that Innis had been given. 'Have you read these?'

He'd already told her about finding the carved stone and what Mr Rivans had discovered about it. 'It's just a story. Every island has a legend about a visit from Bonnie Prince Charlie.'

'But it's all this other stuff, about the challenge and those poor men.'

Innis looked puzzled. 'What stuff is that?'

'Have you read any of it?'

'Not much. I was hoping you could give me the quick version.'

Kat shook her head. 'You are so lazy.'

'It's more your thing. You're into history.'

'Well I didn't know anything about this. And I live on the island.'

'About what? Rivans said he had only told me half the story.'

'The stone you discovered was put there in 1788 by the twelfth Laird of Nin, James MacLeod.'

'That's *old*,' Innis said. 'It must have been tripping people up for centuries.'

'In more ways than you think,' Kat added mysteriously. 'Anyway, the stone was a memorial to mark the death of Bonnie Prince Charlie. As a young man, the twelfth Laird had helped the Prince escape from the government forces. That was part of it, at least. The Laird never married and had no children. Towards the end of his life he became . . .' She squinted at a page in the dark. 'It's described here as, "increasingly eccentric".'

'You mean he went mad?'

'Probably. Definitely, if you consider what happened.'

Kat deliberately left a pause, knowing that it would annoy Innis now that he was intrigued.

'So what happened?'

'Well, James MacLeod decided that he would set a challenge. Successfully complete the challenge and you would inherit the Laird's title, wealth and lands.'

She left it hanging again, teasing him.

'Just tell me.'

'The next Laird of Nin couldn't just be any man. He had to be brave and noble and strong. He had to prove himself worthy. And so a challenge was set. If any man, and it was the eighteenth century so it was only men, no women allowed, if any man could successfully re-enact the Bonnie Laddie's Leap and jump the gap from one side to the other, he would win the prize. And what a prize! There was even a castle.'

'That's just daft,' Innis scoffed. 'I've seen that gap, it's a long way down. No one would even try it.'

'Oh, but they did.' Kat shuffled through the

document until she found the right page. 'A Nin man, a Skye man and an Englishman all tried. They tried and they died. They were –' she searched the document for a quote – '"dashed to pieces on the rocks below".'

'Ouch.'

'Exactly. That was in the first few years after the Laird died in 1790. No one has tried it since, thankfully.'

Innis rested his chin in the cup of his hand. 'But we're from Nin. How come we've never heard of this?'

'I don't know. I guess they hushed it up so no one else would try.'

'You couldn't still do it, could you?'

Kat flipped to the last page. 'According to this, the challenge remains in force until someone successfully crosses the gap and becomes –' she looked for the phrase – '"Lord of the Leap". Until then, the lands and title are being held in trust by a law firm in Edinburgh. Whatever that means.'

'I didn't know Nin even had a Laird.'

Kat gave him a smile. 'Do you fancy being the thirteenth Laird of Nin?'

'Well, I wouldn't mind living in a castle. But as I said, I've seen the leap and you would have to be an idiot to try.'

'Bonnie Prince Charlie did it.'

'Aye, right,' Innis said sarcastically.

'If you'd read the document you would have noticed that the wolves of Nin get a mention.'

'How so?'

'Mr Rivans discovered a page in some old history book. Here's a photocopy – another legend of Bonnie Prince Charlie fleeing across Nin. It says that he only escaped from the soldiers because he was helped by a pack of wolves. The wolves allowed the Prince to pass, recognizing the rightful King of Scotland, and then chased the soldiers into the sea.'

Innis was excited. 'See, I told you there were wolves on Nin.'

'Aye, two hundred and seventy years ago. Not any longer. And it's a legend, not a fact.'

Innis was not to be swayed. 'No, Lachlan and his uncle have brought wolves back to the island.'

Kat gave a harrumph of disbelief. 'Anyway, I think it's dark enough now.'

'We should get back.'

'We could do that. Or we can go and see where Lachlan is living.'

'How do you know that?'

'I saw his pupil profile on my English teacher's computer.' She gave him a sly look. 'Well, she let me use it and forgot to log off. It's hardly my fault.'

'I'm sure you had to click a few times.'

'My hand slipped.' She stood and began walking along the road that ran parallel with the beach. 'Come on then.'

They walked for five minutes until Innis stopped and said, 'There's nothing out here.'

'This is the address,' Kat said, turning 360. 'This is the road.'

Innis stared into the gloom. The breeze was picking up off the ocean and the wind chill was numbing his face. 'Over there, is that something?' Towards the beach there was a faint glow of light.

'Come on,' Kat said, moving past him.

Innis followed, and as they got closer the faint glow became light seeping from a small window.

'It's a caravan,' Kat said.

It *was* a caravan; a small, ancient-looking thing that even in the dark looked rusty and battered. Its wheels were flat and sunk into the ground. It had been a long time since it had moved anywhere.

'Is this where he lives?' Kat whispered.

'Is this where anybody lives?'

'His school profile says he's staying with his older sister and her family. I don't think this can be it.' Again, the mischievous smile appeared. 'But let's knock and see.' She moved up to the door and rapped hard on the rusty metal.

'Kat,' Innis hissed as a clatter came from inside.

They stood in the dark for a few moments, breath held, and then the door opened and light spilled out, making them squint. In the doorway stood the unmistakable, thickset silhouette of Lachlan Geddes.

'What do *you* want?' he barked.

'Do you live here?' she asked.

'What's it to you?'

'I was just wondering.'

'Well, wonder somewhere else.' The boy turned to Innis, standing a few paces back. 'And you. Are you stalking me?'

'No,' Innis said, trying to muster outrage at such an accusation.

'Where's your sister?' Kat asked.

Lachlan's scowl was replaced momentarily by a look of panic. He swiftly rebooted the scowl. 'It's none of your business. None of this is your business.'

'It is if you've lied to the school.'

'And if I've lied to the school how is that your business?'

Innis watched the girl falter for once in offering a reply. It *was* nothing to do with them.

'We're concerned, that's all,' she said.

In what way are we concerned? Innis thought. Nosy? Yes. Meddling? Yes. Concerned? No. He heard Lachlan scoff, as if in agreement.

'When I need your concern, I'll let you know.'

'But you can't live here all by yourself.'

'Who says I'm by myself?'

'You're supposed to be living with your sister and her family. There's no family living here. This thing is barely big enough for you.'

'My sister is away on holiday. She takes long holidays.'

'I don't believe you.'

'In what way do you think that matters to me?'

'Come on, Kat,' Innis said.

'But he's lying.'

'Who cares.'

Innis took a hold of the girl's arm and pulled her back up towards the path.

'And for the last time,' Lachlan shouted after them, 'leave me alone.'

'Or what?' Kat shouted in reply.

The boy slammed shut the caravan door and the whole structure shook.

'"Or what?"' Innis repeated. 'Or he'll murder us and toss our bodies in the ocean.'

Kat shook herself free from his grip. 'You're just scared of him.'

'Aye, I'm scared of him – he's a scary guy.'

Kat stood for a moment and sighed. 'That wasn't much of an adventure, was it?'

'Let's just be glad we escaped alive.'

They began walking back towards the hostel, and as they came within range of the nearest phone mast Kat's phone buzzed. She pulled it from her pocket and checked it as she walked.

'Two missed calls from my mum,' she said. 'And a voicemail.'

She put the phone to her ear and listened, and then halted with a gasp.

'What is it?' Innis asked.

'You better check your phone. It's your grandfather. He's had a fall.'

'Is he all right?'

'He's with my mum tonight but they've called the doctor. You've to catch the first ferry back to Nin in the morning.'

Innis hung his head and groaned. He had feared this day would come. Gramps was supposed to look after him; it couldn't be the other way around. They wouldn't allow it. Especially when he was at school on Skye for most of the week. Up ahead he could see the lights of the hostel. If Gramps didn't get better this might be his home seven days a week. He shuddered at the thought. The hostel was fine but it wasn't his croft, and Skye wasn't Nin. He looked back along the road they had walked but all was dark, except a faint glow from out at sea. If things got really bad, they might bunk him with Lachlan Geddes in that rusty little box that used to be a caravan.

'Gramps will be fine,' Kat said, seeing his anxious face.

'He has to be,' Innis replied, forcing a painful smile. 'I'll have to leave Nin if he's not.'

Chapter 9

Innis sat at the kitchen table and watched the doctor write a prescription. Kat's mum stood in the corner, arms folded. Gramps was resting in his bed.

'I'll increase the dosage of levodopa,' the doctor said, 'which will hopefully make your grandfather steadier on his feet. We'll also get the occupational therapist out again to work with your grandfather on everyday tasks. He fell trying to take washing off the pulley so we'll need to look again at how things are done.'

Kat's mum sighed. 'The number of times I've offered to do his laundry.'

The doctor nodded. 'With an illness like Parkinson's, what patients cling on to most is their independence. John McGarrah is a stubborn man.' He turned to Innis. 'How are the memory lapses?'

Innis stared out the small window. He hated every minute of this. 'They come and go. Some days he's fine, others, well . . .' He couldn't bring himself to say more.

'It's hard lad, I know. And you have to reconcile yourself with the fact that it's not going to get better. Parkinson's is a progressive disease. We will manage it as best we can, but there is no cure.'

Innis nodded. 'How long does he have?'

'Before what?'

'Before he dies.'

'We're not there yet. He could have years to live.'

'How long before he can't stay here any more?'

Innis was really asking about himself.

'That depends on many factors. It's not a decision that has to be made yet. For now, your grandfather is healthy enough. If we all keep an eye on him.'

'Of course we will,' said Kat's mum.

'Are you going back to school?' the doctor asked Innis.

'Not till next week.'

'Good, your grandfather should be on his feet in a day or two. His shoulder and arm are badly bruised but nothing's broken.'

The doctor collected his jacket and hat and left the croft, and Kat's mum departed a few minutes later to feed the baby. She promised to return with soup for lunch. Innis looked in on Gramps, but he was sleeping. He watched his grandfather's chest rise and fall, rise and fall, and his eyes filled with tears. There would come a point in the not too distant future when the breaths would no longer come. Who would want to listen then, while he described the sight of a buzzard soaring high on a summer thermal? Or run him a hot bath when he arrived home after circling the island on his bike? Or make him a plate of mince and tatties covered with ketchup when the ferry got in on a Friday evening?

Who else would tell him everything was fine, when he'd had a day or a week when it hadn't been fine at all?

Only two days later, on Friday morning, Gramps was back to his old self and even the trembling didn't seem so bad. Innis knew Kat would be home later, on the last ferry, and he assumed Lachlan Geddes would be on it as well. That gave him a few hours. The Bonnie Laddie's Leap had been playing on his mind for days now. He wanted another look.

Gramps had encouraged him to get out the house and stop the fussing, so Innis set off on his bike once more. The air was less cold – still not warm, but hats and gloves were no longer required. He cycled along the thin line of black tarmac that circled the island, pedalling and revelling in the fact that everyone was in class right now, except for him. He knew he wasn't being missed. By anyone.

He heard a lapwing offer its distinctive *peewit* call from close by. It was the first of the season and normally he would have stopped for a look – his binoculars were in his backpack – but not this morning. He was on a mission and was not to be diverted. When he reached the track up to the wildlife sanctuary he cycled along the rutted road for a few minutes before stopping and climbing off his bike.

Lachlan Geddes might be at school but his uncle wasn't. Innis would approach with stealth, and that meant cross-country. He hid his bike behind a gorse bush and set off on foot across the moor towards the coast. The ground was firm beneath his feet; it hadn't rained for several days. Spring came late to the island, it was only just getting started, but when it arrived the moorland would burst into colour; red clover and violet butterwort and yellow iris and pink foxglove. And among the moss would be insect-eating sundew plants with sticky tendrils, ready to snare careless midges.

Innis reached the cliff edge a half-mile to the south of the wildlife sanctuary. The ocean was calmer today and he looked across at the Isle of Skye in the distance, picturing Kat in class. He knew her timetable as well as his own; she would be in French, second row from the front, hand in the air with that self-satisfied smile she gave when she knew the answer. Which was all the time.

He began to move north along the cliff edge, but not too close. He didn't like heights and he didn't like water, so a cliff with the ocean at its base was his worst nightmare. It was time, though, to start overcoming some of his fears. He just couldn't decide which one to conquer first.

It took ten minutes to reach the wildlife sanctuary and as he approached the buildings he crept low to the ground. All seemed quiet and there was no smoke from the chimney of the croft. The place seemed locked-up and empty. Innis edged past the buildings and made his way to the point on the coastline where the cliff had a deep cleft. The Bonnie Laddie's Leap.

He moved cautiously to the edge and peered down. This was overcoming a fear. The ocean was less turbulent today but the rocks looked just as jagged. He thought of three bodies lying dashed below, three leapers who hadn't leapt enough. And still the challenge held; if he jumped across the chasm he would be Laird of Nin. What would his teachers and classmates think then?

It was hard to get a sense of the width of the gap, especially with the ocean swirling below, but it didn't seem too far. Innis delved into his backpack and pulled out an old measuring tape borrowed from his grandfather's tool chest. He put one end on the ground at the top of the small inlet and weighed it down with a rock. He then pulled the tape along the back edge of the cleft to the other side, and pinched it at the point where the gap became firm land again. He moved back from the edge and sat down on the grass.

He looked at the tape. A swirl of numbers lifted themselves from the metal strip and juddered before his eyes. His dyscalculia kicking in. He sucked on his bottom lip, narrowed his eyes and focused. He could do this, he could read the measurement. He pulled a pen and small notebook from his backpack and opened it at the first empty page. The rest of the book was filled with observations made on his birdwatching trips across the Barrens; species, numbers, times, weather conditions. The species recordings were perfect. He knew his birds. The counts and timings were less accurate. Often when he looked at his watch it made no sense. Innis focused on the tape again. He carefully wrote *190cm*.

That didn't seem a huge gap. It was hurting his brain thinking about it, but he reckoned that was just over his height. He only had to leap the length of himself and a little extra. Any decent athlete could jump across the Bonnie Laddie's Leap. He wondered why no one had claimed the Lairdship of Nin before now. The gap was bridgeable, the leap was doable. Of course, jumping across firm ground was not quite as pressure-filled as jumping over sure and certain death.

He lay back on the grass and looked up at a sky that was shadowed with grey clouds. An idea was forming in his head.

He would attempt the Bonnie Laddie's Leap.

Innis propped himself up on his elbows and looked at the ocean. For someone whose worst nightmares were heights and deep water, for someone who wasn't especially athletic and whose idea of daring was putting barbecue sauce on his burger instead of ketchup, this was a ridiculous idea. Insane. But that was the beauty of it. He was the last person anyone would expect to attempt such a feat. That would make the 'in your face' all the sweeter.

And if he was Laird of Nin, he thought suddenly, there would be a castle to live in when Gramps became too ill to look after him – his imagination had sparked to life – with servants to take care of them both. How Kat would be impressed – he would no longer be the under-achieving distant relative, the slightly embarrassing next-door neighbour. He lay back on the grass and closed his eyes, could feel his heart beat with excitement. What a thing to do. He would be Innis Munro, adventurer and hero. Innis Munro, Lord of the Leap.

Chapter 10

Innis opened his eyes with the suddenness that comes at the end of a bad dream. He sat up, realizing he must have dozed off as he lay on the clifftop. The clouds had thinned and a hazy afternoon sun brought a brightness to the sky and a shimmer to the ocean.

Something had woken him, an uneasiness that he couldn't place. He felt a tingle run down his spine. Something was firing his senses, setting off his brain's warning bells.

He turned his head slowly until he was looking behind him. And looking into the eyes of a wolf.

It stood a few metres away, legs splayed, head pointing down but eyes fixed on Innis, tail curled under its body. It was a big beast with jet-black fur all over except for two small white patches under each eye. This was no dim silhouette or distant howl. This was a real live wolf, up close.

Innis stopped breathing. The wolf stood silently staring at him. His instinct told him to run, to flee for his life, but he didn't move. He knew he could never outrun a wolf. He knew he was trapped between the animal and the cliff edge. He knew his legs wouldn't work anyway. A fear-induced paralysis was preventing him even taking a breath and his lungs were beginning to burn.

Innis stared into the eyes of the wolf and the wolf peered into the eyes of the boy.

What is it thinking?

He took a breath, because he had to.

Is it as terrified as me?

The wolf didn't look terrified. What kind of wolf was this, with such black fur and yellow, piercing eyes? He thought he should do something, say something perhaps. But what?

'Good wolf,' he said.

The animal gave a startled jolt, turned and ran off towards the buildings of the wildlife sanctuary. It loped up a small slope and disappeared over the top.

Innis lay back on the grass and laughed. Only when his breathing had returned to normal and his legs had stopped shaking did he realize what had just happened. He had come face to face with a real live wolf.

He had been right all along. Lachlan and his uncle were keeping wolves. Too late he remembered the camera in his phone. No one would believe him.

He stood up and looked around him but all was still and quiet. The wolf was gone. He took out his phone anyway and snapped a few pictures of the cliff and the chasm and the carved stone. Then he picked up his backpack and moved cautiously up the hill towards the buildings.

Innis crept under an archway and past a squat building that smelt unpleasantly of some kind of animal. He peered in an open doorway. The room was partitioned by metal grills and each section was piled high with straw, but nothing moved. He walked on, towards the small croft that seemed to be home. It was a house not unlike his own but there were no neatly tended window boxes, no whitewashed walls, no bright-red door with a knocker shaped like a dolphin. This croft had peeling paint on the window frames and walls stained green by moss. There was no pathway to the door, no welcome mat, just two planks of wood that lay in a muddy dip.

He snuck to the back of the croft and peered in a small window. Nothing stirred. He moved around to the front and listened for a growl or a howl but all was quiet. He stood for a moment and his eyes were drawn to the door of the croft. Something was fixed to the warped wood. He moved closer and saw it was a piece of paper with a plastic covering. In bold black letters was written, NOTICE OF EVICTION. Innis quickly scanned the document, saw *final warning* and *thirty day notice* and *withdrawal of lease* and *planning permission* and *wind farm*.

He felt a growing sense of unease. It was time to go. The ferry was due in soon.

Innis cycled down the west side of the island on his return, heading for Skulavaig. It was a small town with only a few shops and cafes, a hotel, two churches, the Fishermen's Mission, a two-room primary school and the harbour.

The Friday evening ferry was the busiest ferry of the week. In summer, it was full of island-hopping tourists. In the third week of March it was just islanders who worked on the mainland returning home, or island teenagers coming back after a week in the school hostel. It was always a happy and excited ferry and Innis was always glad to be on it. He often thought there must be more to life than the island of Nin, but at least when he was home it meant there was a deep, dark body of water between him and school.

He leant on a railing beside the slipway and watched the ferry slowly manoeuvre into position. The water churned, men threw ropes at each other and gulls circled overhead, hopeful of a scrap of something. The ramp slowly lowered and made contact with the concrete slipway with a grating clang. Foot passengers departed first and Innis waited for Kat to emerge from the enclosed passenger deck.

But the smile that burst on his face when he saw her

dark hair and pretty face lasted only a second before he saw the person she was with.

Lachlan Geddes.

Innis watched him lean close to her and say something and they both laughed. Innis had never seen Lachlan smile before; to see him laugh was bizarre. It was like a whole different person and Innis hated Laughing Lachlan even more than he hated Loathsome Lachlan. He felt so betrayed he turned around and walked away at speed. When your friend was a friend of the enemy, then your friend was the enemy too.

Chapter 11

The Barrens felt even more barren than usual. Innis stood on top of a hummock and half-heartedly scanned the moor through his binoculars. He gave a long sigh. It was nine o'clock, too dark now to see anything anyway. If the birds were gone then that left only the wolves. It was time to get home before the howling began.

He tramped across the moorland and as he approached the crofts he saw Kat in her back garden. The telescope was out. He considered giving her a huffy turn of the head as he wandered past but that would just hand Lachlan Geddes a clear run at being her best island friend.

He looked to the heavens. In the dark, clear sky the stars were twinkling with a million points of light.

'Should be a good night for it,' he said.

Kat looked up from her telescope, said with a sigh. 'I suppose so.'

Innis leant on the gate. 'What are you looking for tonight?'

'The Pleiades star cluster.' She added somewhat cryptically, 'While I still can.'

'How was school this week?'

'It was fine. My mum says your grandfather is much better.'

'He's back on his feet, aye.'

'I thought I saw you at the ferry earlier.'

He had been spotted. 'I was in town picking up some things.' It didn't sound convincing but she made no further comment and he pushed the gate open and walked up the path. 'So what's new?' he asked, knowing full well but wanting to hear it from her.

'Nothing much,' she said.

She was going to make him work to get the gossip. 'Did I see you talking with scary Lachlan?'

'He's not so scary when you get to know him.'

'And how well have you got to know him?'

'Just a little bit. He's nice in his own way.'

The betrayal was becoming high treason. 'And what way is that?'

Kat shrugged. 'I don't know. He's interesting to talk to. He has his secrets.'

Secrets didn't make you interesting, secrets made you smug. 'We all have them.'

The girl laughed. 'And what secrets do you have, Innis?'

He wanted to protest but knew his life was an open book, at least as far as Kat was concerned.

The girl sighed and turned away from the telescope. 'Actually, I do have news. Shocking news, in fact.'

This was more like it. He hoped it was something juicy about Lachlan Geddes.

'My dad has just told me, although I'm not supposed to discuss it with anyone. But how can I not?'

Her dad worked for the Highlands and Islands Council. What could he know about Lachlan?

'They're building something on the Barrens,' she said. 'Putting something all over it.'

This wasn't juicy gossip about the scary one. He remembered the document fixed to the door of Lachlan's croft. 'I know,' he said, disappointed. 'A wind farm.'

The girl's jaw dropped. 'How do you know that? My dad says no one knows yet.'

'I just know. It's no big deal.'

'How can you say that? Of course it's a big deal. It will ruin everything. Fifty-eight wind turbines are going to be built, right across the north of the island.'

'I meant it's no big deal how I know. Anyway, isn't wind energy good? It's renewable, it doesn't cause pollution.'

'But it *will* cause pollution – *light* pollution. Each one will be lit up and there will be roads as well, and the roads will have lights.'

She looked up and Innis did the same and they were looking at a black sky awash with shimmering stars. Now he understood.

'It will destroy the dark skies,' Kat said. 'It will ruin everything I've been working for.'

Katrina McColl, despite being only thirteen years old, was vice-chairperson of a small organization of Nin residents who had helped the island become one of Scotland's Dark Sky Discovery Sites. These were places with minimal light pollution, allowing stargazing with the naked eye. With her telescope, Kat could see the furthest constellations. But Kat had grander plans. She was leading the application for Nin to become an International Dark Sky Community. This was a global designation, and much harder to achieve. A town, a city, or in their case an island, had to show 'exceptional dedication to the preservation of the night sky'. That was the wording in the guide from the International Dark-Sky Association, and Kat knew it off by heart.

'What has your dad told you?' Innis asked.

'Nothing much. Just that planning permission has been granted to some big power company and they are putting fifty-eight turbines on to the Barrens, from here all the way up to the lighthouse.'

Innis realized now what the notice at the wildlife sanctuary had meant. The place was being shut down and wind turbines built on the site. That's why Lachlan

Geddes was being evicted. He bit his lip as he tried not to smile.

'When is all this happening?'

'Work begins at the end of the summer.' Kat turned to the boy with a steely resolve in her eyes. 'So we have five months to stop it. Five months to save the dark skies of Nin.'

'That can be your campaign slogan.'

She was excited now. 'Aye, and we're not saying no wind turbines, wind turbines are good, we're saying not on the Barrens.'

Innis pumped an arm in the air. 'Save the Barrens.'

She gave him a stern look. 'This is serious, Innis.'

He nodded. 'Aye, I know.'

'No one loves the Barrens more than you. You're never off them.'

Did he detect a hint of ridicule? Teasing at least. 'Wind turbines are actually very dangerous for birds. They fly into the blades.'

'Exactly. This is bad. We have to save the Barrens.'

Innis had never seen Kat look so worried. 'But how do we do that?'

The girl slowly shook her head and lifted her gaze back up to the stars. Innis looked up as well, and wondered if she thought the answer lay somewhere far out there in the glittering universe.

Chapter 12

'What's the matter lad?' asked Gramps.

Innis was staring out of the small croft window, watching rain bounce off the ground. It always seemed to rain on a Saturday. 'I've just had a text from Mum. She won't be back this weekend after all. There's some big conference on at her hotel.'

Two days earlier, Innis's mum had arrived to check on Gramps, stayed one night and departed on the first morning ferry, satisfied that he was fine. Innis had the sense that his mother was not going to make this a regular occurrence, that if his grandfather's health declined any further then he would have to be moved to the mainland. Innis knew that being away from the island would kill Gramps far quicker than the Parkinson's. He also knew that when Gramps moved, so did he.

'Never mind,' said his grandfather.

Innis could tell that Gramps had forgotten she was supposed to be coming. He lifted himself from his seat and moved to the door of the croft. He opened it and stepped out into the rain.

'You need a jacket,' his grandfather called after him.

'I'm not going far.'

'You'll still get wet.'

'I don't mind.'

Innis climbed up on to the higher land of the moor and stood staring out across the island. In the rain the Barrens shone with a bleakness and a beauty that could not be found anywhere else in the world. And it was all under threat.

Everything. His home. His island. His life.

When Gramps became too ill they would both have to leave, but before that there would be wind turbines to ruin both the landscape he loved and the dark skies that Kat needed for her stargazing.

Innis tilted back his head and let the rain run down his face. There was one way, it seemed, to save the island. And to save himself. An eccentric, long-dead Scottish nobleman had set a challenge which had not yet been completed. The prize was the island of Nin itself.

All he had to do was jump across the Bonnie Laddie's Leap.

Nothing to it.

Except he was a terrible athlete. And there was no

actual proof that the dead Laird's challenge still held true.

He rubbed a hand across his wet face, wiping away the doubts along with the raindrops. He could do this. He could do something unexpected, something remarkable, something... well, yes, something *cool*.

He couldn't remember a time when he had done anything that would be considered in any way cool.

By Saturday lunchtime the rain had relented, and Innis stood by the empty doorway of Nin Castle. It was a half-mile north of his croft, perched on top of cliffs that curved around the south-east portion of Nin. Unlike those on Lachlan's side of the island, these cliffs had a sandy beach at their base and interesting caves in the rock face.

If Innis was to attempt the leap there was something he had to do first. It meant a visit to the castle. Over the three days spent at home with his grandfather, he had finally read all the background information about the Bonnie Laddie's Leap. Included were some detailed instructions about how a leap attempt was to be undertaken. The first step was to post an intention to leap on to the front door of Nin Castle. A door that was no longer there.

The castle was just a ruin. The walls stood tall but the stonework was crumbling and the roof had long ago collapsed. The windows were empty voids of black and every time Innis looked he expected to see a ghostly face staring back. He had always been slightly scared of Nin Castle. He didn't think he would want to live here when he was Laird of Nin.

Innis stood under the stone arch of the doorway. Despite the lack of a door he was still going to post his intention to leap. He was reaching into his backpack to fetch some paper and tape when he heard a clattering of stones from inside the castle. Innis stepped away from the doorway, felt his heartbeat quicken. He had never liked this place.

It was probably just a bird. He pinched his lips together and approached the doorway again, told himself he could look inside without actually going inside. He peered through the stone archway. A pale glow crept through the hole in the roof, but the sky was full of dark clouds that let in little light. There was a large room with rough stone walls and black doorways that led to who knew where. The floor was strewn with fallen stones and deep shadows. High up in the walls, where enough light reached, a few plants clung to the cracks.

Innis looked for a moment and saw movement in the dark. He back-pedalled from the opening and crouched behind a low wall. Something was in the old ruin. He lifted himself slowly from the wet grass where he squatted and peered cautiously over the wall, across what must have once been some kind of courtyard. He stared for a few moments at the doorway. Shadows flickered within the opening and then the face of an animal poked out, sniffing the air.

It was a wolf. The same big one he had seen before, jet-black with patches of white beneath its yellow eyes.

Innis jumped up, pulling his phone from his pocket.

The wolf saw him and for a second it seemed to almost nod its head in recognition. Then it bolted away, disappearing behind the castle remnants that lay scattered around the main structure. Innis snapped a single picture of the retreating animal.

His second close encounter in as many days. He sat down on an old wall and wondered what the wolf was doing so far from the wildlife sanctuary. If it had escaped, it had made it all the way to the other side of island.

Another noise came from inside the castle. Had the wolf doubled back? Innis held his breath, saw movement in the doorway.

A boy emerged through the opening.

It was one of his classmates, one of the island boys. They weren't really friends, but they would exchange a smile on the ferry and nod hello if they met in the school hostel. Usually the boy didn't say much. In fact, he didn't talk at all. The boy's name was Dunny Dunbar.

Innis stood and said, 'Hi, Dunny.'

The boy's dark eyes showed surprise and his eyebrows dipped in a frown beneath hair so blonde it looked white.

Had Dunny seen the wolf? He didn't look as if he'd recently met a wolf face to face.

'What are you up to?' Innis asked.

There was no reply, but he hadn't expected one. Actually, now that the boy was here, he could be useful.

'Can you do me a favour?'

Dunny looked at Innis with suspicion, but he reluctantly nodded.

'I just need you to take a picture of me,' Innis said.

He reached for the backpack that was propped by the doorway. He pulled out a sheet of paper, on to which he had copied the exact wording required in the instructions. All leapers had to first post a proclamation.

I, Innis Munro, a native of the island of Nin, do hereby proclaim and declare that I will endeavour to traverse the clifftop chasm known as the Bonnie Laddie's Leap and will use the vigour of my legs only in this undertaking. I do this under my own volition and at the behest of no man. I do this not for fortune or renown but rather for the immeasurable nobility of the enterprise itself. Upon successful execution of this challenge, I will claim the rewards offered, to wit the Lairdship of Nin and all accompanying lands and titles.

With a piece of tape, he attached the paper to the stone surround of the doorway. He then handed his phone to Dunny and told him to take a picture. Innis stood by the castle entrance and pointed to the proclamation. Dunny snapped a picture.

'Thanks,' Innis said, taking back his phone. 'You're

probably wondering what all this is about.' Dunny shrugged. 'I'm going to attempt something no one has done for over two hundred years. And if I'm successful, this castle will belong to me.'

Dunny's face changed from disinterest to anger. Perhaps he had already taken ownership of the old ruin and didn't appreciate someone else claiming possession. Innis had always been a little wary of Dunny Dunbar. He *was* a little strange.

'Anyway, I will be posting details shortly. Thanks for your help.'

He lifted his backpack and retreated from the castle. It had been a successful visit. He had posted his proclamation *and* bagged a photograph of the wolf roaming the Barrens. No one could deny it now, not even Lachlan Geddes.

Chapter 13

As the Monday morning ferry pulled away from Nin harbour, Innis found himself dangling over the side, the water churning beneath him as his body pressed down on the rail and his fingers gripped tightly to the metal. Lachlan Geddes was trying to tip him out of the boat.

'I hope you can swim!' he heard Lachlan cry.

'Leave him, Lachlan!' he heard Kat cry.

'Let me go!' he heard himself cry.

Lachlan pushed a little more and for a moment Innis thought he really was about to be thrown into the ocean. Then the boy grabbed Innis's jacket and pulled him back from the rail. Innis crumpled in a heap on the deck, panting for breath. He was aware of the other dozen Nin school pupils watching and enjoying the show. A few adults were shaking their heads disapprovingly.

'Do you know what you've done, you stupid idiot?' Lachlan spat.

Kat pulled the angry boy away and Innis propped himself up so he was sitting with his back against the boat's gunwale. His breaths were heavy and his knees were shaking as he watched Kat and Lachlan disappear into the passenger deck. He knew exactly why Lachlan Geddes had lost it.

The previous day, on every social media site he could think of – new ones, old ones, cool ones, lame ones – Innis had posted a picture of the wolf. It wasn't a great one but the secret was out. More importantly, he had posted information and photos of the Bonnie Laddie's Leap, including his proclamation. The reaction so far had been . . . well, underwhelming was one word to describe it. There had been a couple of replies from classmates saying much the same thing:

Eh?

Now, at last, on the ferry, he had got a proper reaction. But not quite the one he had imagined. Kat had slapped him on the shoulder and said, 'Get over yourself.' Then Lachlan Geddes had tried to kill him.

Innis pulled himself to his feet and leant on the rail over which he had almost toppled. Lachlan's reaction had been a little extreme. And what was Kat's problem? He watched the ocean flow past in the wake of the boat, sensed someone standing beside him.

'I bet you're really proud of yourself,' Kat said.

Innis turned slowly. 'You read my post, then.'

'Of course I read your post, it's on about seven different sites.'

'I wanted to make sure no one missed it.'

'Congratulations. The world is now fully aware you're about to die.'

'It's not as far as it looks.'

'Last time you tried to jump a *puddle* your socks got wet.'

'I was wearing the wrong shoes.'

Kat stifled a smile and tried to be cross again. 'You've also been trespassing on the Geddes land, to get your pictures.'

Innis shrugged 'It's not their land. They're about to be evicted.'

'Lachlan says that's not going to happen.'

'You've talked to him about it?'

'Of course. He pretends he's not worried but I know he is. Now, thanks to you, other people will be trespassing on his land, trying that leap thing for themselves.'

'They can't,' Innis said, 'Once someone has posted a proclamation no one is allowed to try until that first attempt has failed. It's in the rules.'

'Yeah, because people follow the rules.'

'Well, they won't become Laird of Nin.'

Kat was frustrated. 'No one is becoming Laird of Nin. That was over two hundred years ago.'

'We'll see.'

'Aye, we'll see you plunge to your death.'

'No, I'll make it to the other side and then I will own the island and we can put the wind turbines somewhere else. That's what you want, isn't it?'

Kat looked as if she was about to cry. 'You can't be doing this for *me*? Please, no. We can stop the wind turbines by organizing protests and writing petitions. We can't do it by you jumping to your death.'

'We'll see,' Innis repeated, not feeling quite as confident. He had hoped Kat might be up for the idea, might help him prepare for the leap. Clearly that was not going to happen.

'You better speak to Lachlan,' she said.

'Why?'

'To apologize.'

'I haven't done anything.'

'You've done plenty.'

'He'll only try and drown me again.'

'He's calmed down. Go and speak to him.' She pushed him in the direction of Lachlan, who was now standing on the other side of the ferry deck, staring out over the ocean.

Innis moved slowly across the boat. Yes, he wanted to talk, but not to apologize.

'You can't deny the wolves now,' he said. 'That's twice I've seen them.'

Lachlan didn't turn around. 'Aye, so you say.'

'You saw the picture I posted.'

Innis watched the boy chew on his bottom lip. 'That's just the rear end of a big black dog. It's not even in focus.'

'It was a wolf. You and I know it.'

'You shouldn't have been on our land.'

'I'm guessing you don't have a licence to keep wolves.'

Lachlan gave a growly sigh. 'There are no wolves in our wildlife sanctuary. But we do have wildcats and other animals. It's bad enough the council are trying to close us down. Now there will be people tramping around, trying to find wolves that don't exist.'

'They do exist. They've escaped and now they're out on the Barrens.'

'Well, you seem to be the only one that's seen them.'

'Tell me about it. There's a big black one that seems to be following me.'

Innis turned his head after a moment and saw that Lachlan was staring at him with a strange look on his face, as if someone had told the boy the answer to a puzzle he didn't understand.

'What?' Innis asked.

'Nothing,' Lachlan snapped, turning back to the ocean.

Innis walked across the deck to where Kat stood.

'Did you apologize?' she asked.

'Lachlan and I have come to an understanding.'

'We can all be friends now?'

'I'm sure we'll be besties.'

'And you're not going to attempt that stupid leap?'

Innis gave a short laugh and looked back towards the island of Nin receding in the distance.

'Oh no,' he said, 'I'm still doing that.'

Chapter 14

Innis first noticed a difference later that morning. As fellow pupils passed by, a few looked at him, one even pointed. Normally he was invisible. In registration class he sat by himself at the back. He stared vacantly out the window and eavesdropped on the conversations of the class.

'Some kind of long jump.'

'You win a prize or something.'

'On Nin, so I won't be going to that.'

'Innis couldn't jump a queue.'

'It will be such an epic fail.'

'It's just a wind-up.'

A louder voice spoke up. 'Right class, what's all the whispering about?'

At this question, Innis turned his focus back to the

room. Mrs Orr was standing with her arms folded, leaning against her desk.

'Is something going on that I need to know about?'

A snigger circled the room like a Mexican wave.

'You need to ask Innis, miss,' said a mouthy girl.

'Well, Innis,' said Mrs Orr, 'is there something you want to tell us?'

Innis felt every eye looking in his direction as a hush fell over the class. 'Not really, miss, it's just something I posted online.'

'Another naked selfie,' said the mouthy girl, and the class laughed.

Innis turned to the girl and placed a hand over his heart. 'You know those photos are for your eyes only.'

The class laughed again.

'Look at his Twitter,' a boy said. 'There's a link posted there.'

'Innis is going to be the next Laird of Nin,' said another girl.

'Is that right?' said Mrs Orr. 'Well, I'm sure it's better than working on a fish farm.'

The class laughed again, and Innis recognized a dig at his island.

'He's jumping over a chasm in a cliff,' said a girl.

'It's called the Bonnie Laddie's Leap,' offered a boy.

Mrs Orr moved back behind her desk and looked straight at Innis with a half-smile. 'Leaping over chasms is only allowed once your homework is finished.'

*

On Tuesday lunchtime, Innis passed the door of Mr Rivans's classroom and heard a shout.

'Innis Munro, a word, if you please.'

He backtracked and entered the room. Mr Rivans was sitting at his desk, a peculiar smile on his face.

'Well lad,' the teacher said, 'I see you're trying to make a bit of history of your own.'

'You've heard?'

'You're the talk of the school.'

'Really?' The thought gave Innis a nice feeling inside. He was the talk of the school. But what kind of talk? 'Is everyone saying I'm an idiot?'

'Not everyone.' Mr Rivans smiled. 'Well, aye, pretty much everyone. But they dinnae understand, do they, lad?'

'Understand what?'

'The historical significance of what you're about to do. And the honour involved. You've read the proclamation. You leap for the *immeasurable nobility of the enterprise itself.*'

'I don't really understand what that means,' Innis said.

Mr Rivans laughed. 'It means if you leap out of greed, for just the fortune or the fame, then you are doomed to fail. There has to be a higher purpose to your leap.' His face took on a very serious look. 'Is there a higher purpose to your leap, laddie?'

'I think so,' Innis said hesitantly, still not sure if he completely understood. 'They want to put wind turbines across my island and if I do the leap I can stop it happening.'

Mr Rivans clapped his hands together. 'Well then my lad, you are destined to succeed. You will be the next Laird of Nin.'

'But it was all such a long time ago. Does it still count?'

Mr Rivans rose from his desk.

'Oh aye, it still counts. Your talk of the Bonnie Laddie's Leap was a wee puzzle and I do enjoy a good history mystery. I contacted the lawyers in Edinburgh last week. They took a few days to get back to me, no one in their office had heard anything about it, but they found the original legal documentation in some dusty file somewhere. As far as they can tell, there was no time limit set on the challenge. You leap the leap and you get the island. The common land anyway, the bits that don't belong to other people.' There was a sparkle in the man's eye as he moved closer. 'There is definitely a title, Laird of Nin, but it is not a title of nobility I'm afraid, there is no peerage attached. A laird ranks below a baron, but above a gentleman. You will also inherit the castle.'

Innis didn't have a clue what Mr Rivans was talking about, but whatever it was it seemed good news. 'The castle is just a ruin,' he said.

'That disnae matter. It's still a castle.'

'So you don't think I'm an idiot?' Innis asked.

The teacher laughed. 'I would try it myself if the old legs didnae creak so much.'

On Wednesday evening Innis sat alone in the hostel common room, waiting for the bell to ring for dinner. It was good to be by himself for a few minutes. It felt like the only two people in school he had not talked to were Katrina McColl and Lachlan Geddes. He wondered if they had spent the day together. He hoped Kat was too busy studying and that Lachlan had bunked off again.

Innis stared through the window as swirly rain rattled the glass. His mind was occupied by two thoughts; the leap and the wolves. He wasn't completely certain that either of them was real.

A girl stuck her head in the room. 'There's someone at the door for you.'

Innis lifted himself from his seat and moved to the door, puzzled by who would be visiting at this time of evening. At the front door stood a young woman. She wore a thick rain jacket, but the hood was down and her long blonde hair was bedraggled. She looked cold.

'Can I help you?' Innis asked.

'Innis, hello,' she said. 'My name is Lucy McKenzie.' She offered her hand and Innis shook it with puzzled hesitation. 'I'm a reporter with the *Western Isles Gazette*.'

'The newspaper?' The young woman nodded and Innis added, 'My grandfather reads it sometimes.'

'Well, we're always looking for good local interest stories and your Bonnie Laddie's Leap certainly fits the bill.'

'You're putting it in the paper?'

'If you will allow us, yes. It will be our exclusive.'

Innis had pictured himself on a front cover at some point, but in his mind it was *National Geographic*. He supposed the *Western Isles Gazette* would have to do for now.

'How do you know about it?' he asked.

'I have a cousin who's in his last year at your school. He keeps his ear to the ground for me.'

Innis smiled. *They know me in the senior school as well*, he thought. He noticed again that the woman looked cold. 'We're not really supposed to have visitors but if it's only for a minute.' He held open the front door and beckoned her in.

'I just need a little background information. And a picture as well. It won't be in the newspaper until next week but it will be on our website later tonight.'

Innis showed the reporter into the common room and from her jacket pocket she lifted out a notepad, pen and her phone. 'I'll take notes and record at the same time if that's okay.'

'Sure, whatever.' He sat in a chair opposite the woman.

'So, tell me,' she gave him a wide-eyed grin, 'how do you plan to avoid a horrible death at the bottom of a cliff?'

Chapter 15

By Thursday lunchtime, Innis was outside the head teacher's office, perched on the edge of a long wooden bench polished to a shine by a thousand fidgety bottoms nervously awaiting their fate. Mr MacDonald had requested Innis's attendance immediately after the lunch bell.

The door opened and a stern face poked out. 'Innis, come in please.'

Innis followed the head teacher into the office. A single plastic chair sat in front of a large desk. The man pointed to the chair and Innis sat down. Mr MacDonald lowered himself into a padded swivel chair, which squeaked satisfactorily. He stared for a few moments at a computer screen and said, with a pause between each word, 'So. Then. Innis.' His head turned slowly until he was looking at the boy, and his hand rose and waved vaguely towards the screen. 'We can't be having this.'

Mr MacDonald was a small, tubby man with very little hair, but he had a presence which filled a room like a bear standing on its hind legs.

'Can't be having what, sir?'

The head teacher sprang to life, rising from his chair with arms raised. 'This Bonnie Laddie's Leap nonsense. Right there on the *Gazette* website: *Local pupil to throw himself off a cliff while the world watches.*' The man's eyes narrowed. 'I don't think so, laddie.'

'That's not what the headline says.'

Mr MacDonald's voice was raised. 'It might as well be.'

Innis took a breath. Normally he wouldn't dare answer back but he couldn't allow his leap attempt to be banned simply because the head teacher didn't want bad publicity.

'With respect sir, you can't stop me.'

Mr MacDonald's body jolted at such insubordination. 'What do you mean?' He raised his small frame up and puffed out his chest. 'Of course I can stop you. You are a pupil at this school and what you do reflects on this school. I forbid it.'

Innis took another breath. He would be the calm one. 'This is nothing to do with school. You *can't* forbid it. I'll do it during the school holidays. It will be on my own island. It's my choice.'

The head teacher was bristling now. 'But you are just a child. You don't have a choice. You do as you are told.'

'I'm thirteen and that is old enough to make important decisions about *my* life. And when I'm not in school it's my grandfather who tells me what to do, not you.' Innis slunk down in the chair.

'Is that right? Well, unfortunately for you, at the moment we *are* in school and so *I* will be telling you what to do. So let's begin with detention. For a week. Lunchtime and after school.' Mr MacDonald pointed to the door. 'Collect your lunch and report to the detention room.'

Innis stood. 'Yes, sir.' He walked towards the door and breathed a silent sigh of relief. If the worst of it was detention then that wasn't so bad. His head teacher couldn't stop the leap and had just admitted as much.

On Thursday evening the big gun was wheeled out. His mother. The door of his hostel room was flung open and in strode Moira Munro. Innis sat up on his bed and pulled the headphones away from his ears. He could tell his mum was fizzing.

'I'm supposed to be at work, you know.'

His mother was dressed in her hotel uniform. Her assistant manager badge glinted in the pale sun coming through the window.

'Why are you here, Mum? Is Gramps all right?'

'Your grandfather is fine. Although he won't be if he finds out about this nonsense. Have you told him yet?'

Innis looked sheepishly to the floor. 'I haven't mentioned it, no.'

'Just as well.' Moira Munro's voice softened and she sat on the end of his bed. 'What are you playing at, son?'

'I'm not playing at anything. It's not a game.'

'But you can't be serious about doing this leap. It's far too dangerous.'

'It's just a challenge. It's really not that difficult.'

'If it's not that difficult why has no one done it by now?'

'No one knew about it. It was a big secret.'

'And why was that?' asked his mum, as if proving a point.

They sat in silence for a few moments. The reality was his mum had turned over parenting duties to Gramps in the last few years, and when she tried to take them back again it always felt awkward, as if she should apologize first for not being around much.

'Have you talked to anyone?' she asked. 'The school psychologist, for instance.'

Innis snorted. 'This is not a cry for help, Mum. And I'm not attention-seeking, although it is nice to get it. I am certainly not trying to kill myself. It is not my intention to die in the attempt.'

'But it is quite a distance,' said his mum, 'and others *have* died trying.'

'It's not that far.' He remembered what Mr Rivans had said. 'And the men who died were leaping for the wrong reason. They had no higher purpose.'

He looked at his mum and could see she didn't understand. He offered a smile. 'Plus, it was a long time ago. They had the wrong type of shoes.'

There was no smile from his mum. 'If your father was here he would put you straight. You never listen to me.'

'Well, Dad is in the Gulf of Thailand and won't be back till summer.'

His mum said, very quietly, 'You'll be dead by then.'

'No I won't. I intend to train and practise and I *will* make it to the other side. I'm not suicidal. And I'm not delusional.'

'No, you're just daft.'

In the uncomfortable silence that followed Innis saw his mother's distraught face and knew what had to be done. He could defy his head teacher but he couldn't disappoint his mum. The Bonnie Laddie's Leap was over.

He was about to tell her as much when her eyes tightened and she said, 'How about this, then. You tell your grandfather everything he needs to know about this leap. And then you take his advice. If Gramps tells you not to do it, you don't do it. You must promise me.'

'Okay,' Innis said. He gave a silent shout of triumph. The leap was saved, his grandfather could be convinced. He gave a pretend sigh and put on a dejected, defeated voice. 'We'll let Gramps decide. He'll know best.'

Innis watched the ramp of the ferry slowly descend. It

was Friday afternoon, and he was glad to be heading home. It had been the craziest week ever. He had been mocked by many, admired by a few. He suspected most hoped to see him fail but at least now people knew he existed.

As the cars began to depart from the ferry he looked around and saw Kat talking to another girl. He hadn't seen Kat since Wednesday, which only added to the strangeness of the week. Usually they spent time together every day. That would normally have resulted in gossip, but because they were cousins no one seemed to bother. Or was it because everyone assumed Kat could do a lot better than him?

Innis looked for Lachlan Geddes. There was no sign of the boy and he hadn't been in school today. Innis guessed he was already back on Nin.

The foot passengers were beginning to move on to the ferry and Innis lifted his back pack and a big bag full of dirty washing. He was halted by his name.

'Innis Munro.'

He turned to see a man moving towards the slipway. He was young, with a short beard and long hair.

'I'm glad I caught you,' he said as he arrived. 'How are you doing?'

'Fine,' Innis replied suspiciously. He still had to be wary of strangers, despite his new-found fame.

'You don't know me—' the man began.

'I don't,' Innis interrupted, backing away. 'And I'm

heading home now.'

'I have a proposal for you,' the man said, following.

'Do you have a ticket?'

'For what?'

'The boat.'

The man seemed to notice the ferry for the first time. He stopped and Innis kept moving.

'This could make you a lot of money Innis,' he said. 'Even if you don't make the leap, even if you fail, you'll still get the money.'

Nice vote of confidence, Innis thought. 'I have to go.'

'Okay, we'll talk later.' The man was shouting now. 'Check us out though. Aff yer heid dot com. All one word.'

Innis walked up the ramp and moved to the bow of the ferry. He stood by himself at the rail and stayed there for the whole sailing, despite the cold wind, watching Nin slowly fill the horizon. The attention he was getting was great and he intended to lap up every minute of it, but right now all he needed was the peace and quiet of the Barrens. There were no people on the Barrens. Only birds, deer and the occasional wolf.

Chapter 16

'I'm ready to press on if you are,' Gramps said.

'Are you sure? We can easily go back,' said Innis.

His grandfather slowly raised himself to his feet from the rock on which he was resting. 'I'm fine. I just needed a wee sit down.'

Innis stood as well, and placed the water bottle back in the pocket of his backpack. He looked around him. They were in the middle of the Barrens and it was just him and his grandfather, just like old times. Gramps was having one of his 'good days'. The spring sun was warm on their faces, the air was cool and clean and it was wonderfully quiet. The yellow of the gorse and the purple of the heather added colour to the greeny-brown of grass and moss. From somewhere close by came a sharp *queep*, *queep* call.

'That's a ringed plover,' Gramps said. 'It can see us coming.'

Innis lifted his binoculars and scanned the ground ahead and, sure enough, a small bird broke cover. Grey wings, a white breast and a band of black around its neck.

'There it is,' he said, and Gramps simply answered, 'Aye,' as if he knew already where it would be.

Innis never failed to be amazed at his grandfather's ability to recognize a bird from its call or song. Innis had an app on his phone now, which helped him identify different species, but he needed to see the feathers. It was Gramps who had introduced him to birdwatching during their long treks across the island. As Innis had moved from age ten to eleven to twelve his legs had stretched, and he could keep up easier. He thought that by the time he was a teenager he would be leading the way but before he turned thirteen Gramps had been diagnosed with Parkinson's disease. Innis had resigned himself to the fact that there would be no more walks across the Barrens with his grandfather. But this Saturday morning he had been shaken awake and told to get his boots on. They were going in search of golden eagles.

Innis watched Gramps as he stepped carefully across the hummocky ground, using walking poles for support when necessary.

'We could have lunch here,' Innis said.

'No, no, lunch at the mountain.'

'Are you sure you can walk that far?'

His grandfather stopped and turned. 'I told you lad, today is a good day and lately there have been more bad than good. The disease comes and goes and when you're feeling on top of it, like today, you have to make the most of it.'

'But last week you couldn't get out of bed.'

'And this week I'm better. Come on.'

Gramps moved on and Innis followed. The pace was slower than before the disease and his grandfather paused for breath frequently, but gradually *Beinn Ainmhidhean,* the Hill of the Beasts, began to loom above them.

As they reached the foot of the mountain, Gramps stopped and leant against a large fallen boulder.

'I've missed this place,' he said.

'No sign of the birds,' Innis said, looking upwards through his binoculars.

'They'll be away hunting.'

'Time we had something to eat as well.'

'Aye, but let's go up to our spot.' Halfway up the mountain was a stone ledge where they used to sit and eat and admire the view.

'We can't climb up there Gramps, you're not fit enough.'

'I'm fine lad. It's not far.'

His grandfather took off, digging his poles into the ground and bending his back as the grassy ground began to slope upwards.

'Take your time,' Innis said, hurrying after his grandfather.

He caught him up and took his arm and together they climbed. The ground was firm and with the sun at their back they made it to the rocky ledge. Innis helped his grandfather into a sitting position with his legs over the edge and his back against the face of a small crag. He could tell that Gramps was done in, that the man had overestimated his strength, but they were here now and could rest awhile.

'Will you look at that,' Gramps said, gazing out across the island.

They could see all the way to the ocean that sparkled in the sunlight. To the north were a series of grassy hills that stretched up to the road and the lighthouse. To the west, on the horizon, were the mountains of Skye. To the south, in the far distance across the moor, was Nin Castle and the town of Skulavaig.

'Aye, it's a bonny view,' said his grandfather.

Innis handed him a sandwich from the backpack and took one for himself. They sat eating in silence and Innis felt a calm that he hadn't felt in over a week. As he looked across the Barrens, he could see the edge of the island in the distance and knew that over there somewhere lay the Bonnie Laddie's Leap. He had promised his mum that he would raise the subject with his grandfather but he didn't know where to begin. *Gramps, I'm planning to jump off a cliff. What do you think?* It wasn't a good opening, but he could think of none better. He ate another sandwich.

'So, what's new with you, lad?' asked his grandfather after a while.

Everything, Innis thought, *absolutely everything.* 'Nothing much,' he said.

'Is that right?' Gramps took a couple of bites from an apple. 'I was talking to Katrina's mother. And then *your* mother phoned.'

Innis swallowed his last bit of sandwich. His grandfather knew. 'What were they saying?'

'I think you know, lad.'

Innis sighed. 'About the leap.'

'Aye.'

'I can make it to the other side.'

'Are you sure?'

'It isn't that far, less than two metres. You just need to have the courage to go for it.'

'And do you have the courage, lad?'

'I think so.' Innis saw his grandfather's look. 'I definitely do.'

'But why try it in the first place?

'If I make it I become Laird of Nin.'

'If?'

'*When* I make it I become Laird of Nin.'

'And why do you want to be Laird of Nin?'

This was the grilling Innis knew was coming. Somehow he had to convince his grandfather.

'If I'm Laird of Nin I can save the island.' He gave a sweep of his arm. 'I can save this place.'

'Save it from what?'

'They're building wind turbines all across the Barrens. Fifty-eight of them.'

Gramps nodded. 'Aye, I heard that. It explains the men in yellow jackets I've seen tramping about the moor.'

'It will destroy this place. Our place. And it will chase away the birds. And it will ruin the dark skies that Kat needs for her stargazing.'

'It will be a pity, aye. I've nothing against wind turbines but the Barrens isnae the spot for them.'

'Well, I can stop them. If I'm Laird of Nin then the Barrens will belong to me.'

His grandfather chuckled. 'I'm not so sure about that.'

'Well, I will be able to do *something*.'

'You're only thirteen, laddie.'

'That won't matter. I'll be the boy that leapt the Bonnie Laddie's Leap.'

Gramps made a sound somewhere between a snort and a laugh. 'That *will* be quite a thing.'

Innis sat in silence with his grandfather and they looked out over the rugged grandeur that lay before them. An isolated moor that stretched to the edge of a small island that lay on the edge of a northerly kingdom that sat on the edge of a vast continent. It was a land unchanged in centuries, millennia even, not since the ice sheets had melted and left behind the hills and glens and lochs. And now a horde of metal masts were going to for ever transform this place that he loved. In a very real way, Innis felt that the Barrens belonged to him already, that the place had always been his.

'Well, if you think you can do it,' his grandfather said.

Innis caught his breath and wondered if he had heard right. 'You're not going to stop me?'

'You're a sensible lad. I'm assuming you wouldnae do it if there was a chance you might die. You cannae leave old Gramps alone in the world.'

'I would never do that.'

Innis wanted to tell Gramps the other reason he was doing it, the most important one; that his grandfather would never have to leave the island. But he knew Gramps wouldn't allow it if *that* was the purpose.

'Thank you,' he said quietly. 'I won't let you down.'

'You never have, lad.'

There was silence for a few moments and Innis felt his eyes fill with tears. Tears of excitement that permission had come, tears also of dread now there was no going back, tears mostly of love that he felt for his grandfather. He looked through his binoculars, so Gramps wouldn't see his watery eyes.

At the bottom of the hill he saw some movement. He shifted his binoculars back to the spot for a better look. It took a few seconds until he found it again. He took a sharp breath and sensed his grandfather's head turn towards him.

'A wolf,' he whispered.

He looked at Gramps and saw a frown of disbelief.

'Down there.' Innis pointed and handed over the binoculars.

His grandfather searched the ground for a moment. 'It cannae be a wolf, lad. Are you sure?'

'It has black fur. It's walking slowly towards us.' Innis wanted the binoculars again but Gramps was moving them carefully back and forth.

Then his grandfather exclaimed, 'Oh my goodness!'

'Do you see it?'

'I do.' The man shook his head. 'That's a wolf all right.'

Gramps handed back the binoculars. Innis scanned the hill but couldn't find the animal. He moved his focus in the other direction, saw a second wolf. Its fur was just as black.

'There's two of them,' he said.

'Oh my,' said Gramps. 'Are those the animals from the wildlife sanctuary?'

'They've escaped. They're just roaming the Barrens.'

A question formed in Innis's mind as he focused again on the second one.

Had they escaped, or had they been released?

The second wolf was sniffing the ground, moving in a slow circle. Innis shifted his binoculars again and his eyes came to rest on a third wolf. It was the big one he'd seen before.

He could feel his heart beat fast and suddenly his mouth felt as dry as a sand dune.

'There are three wolves.'

He looked again at the big one and the animal lifted its gaze and stared straight at him. Its top lip curled back to display a row of sharp teeth. Innis dropped the binoculars in fright. He felt a nudge on his arm.

'Over there,' his grandfather said quietly.

Innis looked to where his grandfather pointed, to their left at the bottom of the hill. Binoculars weren't needed this time. A fourth wolf was moving up the slope towards them.

'It's a pack,' Innis said.

'This isnae good.' His grandfather stood quickly and lifted his walking poles. He gave one to Innis.

'Come on,' he said, 'we have to go higher. Claim the high ground.'

'What's happening?' Innis asked, a tremble in his voice.

'The wolves are hunting. They're coming up the hill.' His grandfather brandished his walking pole like a club.

'They're coming for us.'

Chapter 17

Gramps moved slowly up the mountain, the old man digging his hands into the grass and pulling his frail body higher. Innis turned to face the wolves but there was no sign of the animals.

'Come on, lad,' he heard his grandfather call.

Innis chased after him and took the old man's arm when he caught up. His grandfather was wheezing.

'I can't see the wolves,' Innis said.

'We need to get up to that rocky ledge.'

'We'll never make it.'

'Just keep moving.'

Innis looked down, but again there was nothing. He pulled on his grandfather's arm. Gramps was struggling and in pain. They climbed slowly and Innis imagined the wolves advancing much faster, circling unseen to surround them and move in for the kill. The thought made his legs drive even harder up the slope.

'How are you doing, Gramps?' he asked.

His grandfather nodded, didn't have the energy to speak, his eyes to the ground, marking out where his next unsteady step should be. It took all of Innis's strength to drag his grandfather the last few steep metres.

'We're nearly there,' Innis gasped. He glanced behind him, expecting the wolves to be upon them. *They're hunting,* he thought, *we won't see them until the last second…*

They had made it to the highest point they could reach. Innis helped his grandfather down to a sitting position, his back against the rock wall. Gramps was deathly pale and his breaths were laboured. Innis was suddenly terrified he would die of a heart attack before the wolves even reached them. He grabbed both walking sticks. He was angry now, angry at what the wolves had done to his grandfather, angry also at idiot Lachlan for having so little control over them. *Let them come,* he thought. He whipped the walking poles through the air, as if he was eight again and wielding his lightsabers.

Show yourself.

Almost immediately he got his wish. The big wolf with the distinctive white patches emerged from behind a rock. It loped round the mountain, moving slowly upwards. Innis felt his boldness wither. The big wolf was followed a moment later by a smaller one. Innis stepped across the ledge and peered down below. A third wolf was standing, looking up, its tongue hanging from its mouth as if licking its lips.

'Here they come,' he said quietly. He sensed his grandfather trying to lift himself up. 'It's okay Gramps, I've got this.' He gripped the poles tightly and swallowed hard.

Something else moved down below. It wasn't a wolf this time. It was a red deer, its newly budded antlers still rounded at the tips. The young stag stopped suddenly, as if it had only now noticed a wolf pack on the mountain.

Innis grabbed his binoculars for a better look, and said to his grandfather, 'The wolves aren't hunting us. They're hunting a deer.'

Gramps gave a wheezy chuckle and slumped back against the rock face. Through the binoculars, Innis watched the deer turn and run. With a sudden movement, the predators were in pursuit. He counted five black wolves, spread out behind the deer, working as a pack with the big one in front. The deer disappeared around the curve of the mountain and the wolves followed, moving out of sight.

Innis gave the deepest of sighs and dropped the remaining pole he was holding. 'They're gone.'

In a voice that was just a whisper, his grandfather said, 'I really thought they were coming for us.'

Innis crouched down, unable to shake the feeling that the wolves *had* been coming for them, and that the deer had been a lucky distraction. 'How are you feeling?'

The old man nodded, said only, 'I'm tired.'

Innis gave him a drink of water. He saw his grandfather's arm shake as the bottle was lifted to his lips.

'We need to get you home now.'

'A cup of tea would be nice.' The old man gave his grandson an apologetic smile.

Innis pulled out his phone, but there was no reception here at the centre of the island. This was not the place to be stuck, on the highest point on Nin with an ailing old man and no way down. Even if they got to the bottom, it was too far for Gramps to walk back home in his condition. He could go for help but that would mean leaving his grandfather alone to face the wolves. If they failed in the deer hunt they might come looking for easier prey.

'Can you try and walk a little?' he asked.

'Maybe in a wee minute,' said his grandfather, taking slow breaths.

Innis looked across the island, saw clouds and a darkening sky. They didn't have a wee minute. What to do? He couldn't think straight. He had to go and fetch help but he couldn't leave his grandfather. He couldn't leave his grandfather but he *had* to go fetch help.

From the other side of the bluff came the sound of rocks tumbling down scree. Something was on the move and coming their way. Innis lifted a walking pole with one hand and picked up a large stone with the other. He turned to face what was coming, waited for a wolf to appear from behind the rock. He breathed hard, heard a noise, saw movement, raised his pole, readied himself for the wolf, was ready to strike . . .

'Whoa!' said Lachlan Geddes, appearing from behind the outcrop.

'You!' Innis dropped the pole and stone. He bent double, clutching his knees, thinking he was going to be sick.

'What are you doing up here?' Lachlan asked.

'We were being chased by your wolves.' Innis straightened and tried to control his breathing.

Lachlan looked at Gramps. 'Who's that?'

'He's my grandfather.'

'Is he all right?'

'Not really, no.'

'What's wrong with him?'

'He's exhausted. He has Parkinson's disease.'

'What's that?'

'It's a disease of the nervous system.'

Gramps was sitting quietly against the rock, eyes closed. Both arms had an obvious shake.

'Do you need help?'

Innis nodded. 'I don't know how we're going to get back.'

Lachlan stood for a moment, thinking. 'If we can get your grandfather down to the bottom of the mountain I can take him to the road on the quad bike.'

'Once we're at the road Kat's mum could come and collect us.'

'Let's go then.'

Lachlan stepped forwards, but was halted by Innis's raised arm.

'Wait. On Monday you tried to throw me off the ferry. Now you're being nice to me. What's going on?'

Lachlan's face took on a sneer, as if the boy had suddenly remembered who he was.

'Don't think because I'm trying to help your sick grandfather that I'm being nice. If it was just you I would leave you here on the mountain to rot.' He stepped past Innis and went to help Gramps, spoke with quiet menace over his shoulder. 'Get it into your thick head – I don't do nice.'

Chapter 18

The rain had started, a misty smirr of wind and water.

'Can you walk, Gramps?' Innis asked.

The old man gave a smile. 'I'll have to if I want to get off this mountain.'

'That's the spirit,' Lachlan said.

With help, Innis's grandfather lifted himself to his feet.

'We could always call for the coastguard helicopter,' said Innis.

Gramps snorted. 'Dinnae be daft. I've climbed this mountain a thousand times and I havenae been winched off it yet.' He shrugged away Innis's supporting hands. 'Fetch me those poles.'

Carefully, with Innis and Lachlan on either side, the

old man began to move down the side of the mountain. The rest seemed to have given him fresh energy and his hands trembled only slightly as he gripped the walking poles. Innis took a gentle hold of his grandfather's elbow and helped steady him and soon they were off the steep part. After twenty minutes of slow descending the ground levelled off and they reached the bottom of the slope.

Lachlan's quad bike was there.

'Well done, Gramps,' Innis said.

'Nothing to it.' His grandfather gave a painful smile that momentarily brightened a face creased with exhaustion.

Innis pulled out his phone, and was surprised to see that he had reception now. It came and went like the clouds. He called the McColls and talked on the phone for a minute, then said, 'They're going to meet us at the lighthouse.'

Innis looked at the quad bike. At one time it had been green, but now it was coated with a layer of brown mud spreading up from the four wide wheels. The black leather of the seat was cracked, and attached to the back was a metal trailer with a low grill around it.

'Gramps can't go in there,' Innis said, nodding to the trailer.

'Your grandfather is sitting up beside me. The trailer is damp and uncomfortable and covered in animal crap. That's for you to ride in.'

'I think I'll walk.'

'You'll never keep up and you need to stay with your grandfather.' The boy smiled. 'In you get.'

Lachlan sat on the quad bike and scrunched forwards so that Innis could help his grandfather on to the seat behind him. The old man gripped a metal bar at his back.

'Can you hold on there?' Innis asked.

'I'm not decrepit lad, there's still a bit of life in me.'

Innis threw the backpack and poles into the trailer and jumped in himself. He hunkered down at the front, where it seemed least stained. Lachlan started the engine and gently pushed on the throttle. The quad started moving, the boy keeping it slow and steady. The trailer still bounced across the ground and Innis gripped tight to the edge, trying not to yell every time his bottom banged hard against the floor.

'Are you okay, Gramps?' he shouted above the roar of the engine, the fumes from the exhaust making him queasy.

His grandfather didn't turn around, just gave a nonchalant wave as if to say, *Look, I can do this one-handed.* The rain still swirled and Innis felt the cold seep beneath his jacket. After a bumpy ten minutes the horizon began to open up and Innis knew they were approaching the coast. Ahead he could see the top of the lighthouse that sat at the northern tip of the island. The lantern had come on in the early evening gloom and the beacon seemed to be calling them home as it flashed every few seconds.

Finally, the quad bike bumped off the moor on to hard road. Lachlan turned west and drove for a minute more before turning on to a track that led down to the lighthouse. A Land Rover was parked on the road and both Kat and her mum stepped out of the vehicle as the quad bike came to a stop. With her long brown hair, Kat's mother looked just like an older version of her daughter, especially when they wore the same facial expression. They were both frowning.

'Are you all right, John?' Mrs McColl asked.

Innis jumped out of the trailer and helped his grandfather from the bike.

'I'm fine, lass,' the old man said. 'Just overdid it a wee bit.'

'Not half.' The woman looked at Innis with scorn. 'What were you thinking, Innis, dragging your grandfather across half the island and then making him climb a mountain? How could you be so foolish and so selfish?'

Innis watched Kat nod her head in agreement. Was this about his grandfather or was this about the leap? Lachlan moved to stand beside the girl, smirking. Innis opened his mouth to protest then shut it just as quick. It was pointless defending himself, in the end it *was* his fault.

'Dinnae blame the lad,' his grandfather said by way of rescue. 'It was my idea to go for a walk.'

Kat's mum tutted. 'That disnae mean Innis should

have encouraged you.' She looked again at Innis. 'You're supposed to be looking after him, not indulging his foolish whims.'

The old man laid a gentle hand on the arm of the woman. 'No, lass. I'm the one who is looking after Innis. He's just a boy, dinnae forget.'

Kat's mum shook her head and ushered Gramps into the warmth of the Land Rover. Innis stood and considered the harsh reality. His grandfather was the carer, not the other way around. What would happen when the job became too much for the old man?

'Are you coming?' he heard Kat say.

He looked up and she was standing with the passenger door open, the frown back on her face. It only lifted when she turned to Lachlan.

'Thanks. I think you saved the day.' She gave a disappointed glance in Innis's direction then pulled herself into the vehicle.

Innis trudged over and said with effort, 'Aye, thanks.'

'No problem,' said Lachlan with a smug smile.

Innis felt the strongest urge to smack the boy, but knew he would only get a pounding in return. 'Believe me,' he said, 'I know exactly what's going on with the wolves.'

Lachlan looked troubled. 'What do you mean by that?'

Kat called from inside the vehicle, 'Come on Innis, we need to go.'

Innis leant in towards Lachlan and said quietly,

'Well, I'm certain you don't have permission to keep a pack of wolves. And there is no way you would allow them to escape so frequently. If you wanted to keep them penned, you would. No, the wolves haven't escaped, they've been freed. You've released a pack of wolves on to our island.'

The colour drained from Lachlan's face and he looked angry and afraid at the same time.

'Thanks for the ride,' Innis said, pulling shut the door.

The Land Rover pulled away up the track towards the main road. Innis turned around and looked back, watched Lachlan Geddes stand with his arms by his side, a look of fury on his face. The release of the wolves had just been a hunch, but Innis knew now it was true.

By Sunday morning the rain had disappeared and the sun shone in a cloudless sky. It was a low, cool sun, but it still felt good as Innis stood with his chin raised and eyes closed, his face bathed in its rays. Summer felt a long way away. He opened his eyes and knocked on Kat's door. He had given her the morning to attend church and have lunch. Her oldest brother opened the door, gave him the once over and shouted 'Kat', before disappearing back inside. Kat's brothers were not overly fond of their distant relative and not-distant-enough neighbour. Innis didn't play shinty and didn't fish and didn't throw rocks at seagulls. Kat's brothers found it vaguely embarrassing that they shared great-great-grandparents.

Kat appeared at the door. 'What do you want?' she said abruptly.

'For you to be nice to me again.'

For a moment the girl was stumped for a reply. 'Well, you're an idiot,' she said eventually.

'In what way, exactly?'

'You almost killed your grandfather.'

'I thought we had covered that subject yesterday?'

'You're trying to kill yourself.'

'How so?'

'That stupid leap. If that's not being an idiot I don't know what is.'

'No one can say the word leap without adding the word *stupid*. It's not my plan to kill myself. I measured it. It's not so far.'

Kat just shook her head. 'Why are you here?'

'Have you seen what's happening up on the Barrens?'

'What?'

'Come and see.'

She hesitated. 'What is it?'

'Come and see.'

The girl sighed but went back indoors to put on her boots and jacket. When she reappeared, Innis was already waiting on the higher land above their crofts. Kat pulled herself up beside him and looked out over the bleak landscape.

She gasped. 'What are they doing?'

In the distance, two men stood beside a large yellow tripod that held an instrument with an eye piece. One of them was staring through the viewfinder. They wore hi-vis jackets and hard hats.

'Let's go and ask,' Innis said.

As they approached, one of the men said, 'You kids need to go back.' His accent was English, not of the island.

'We live here,' Kat said indignantly. 'What are you doing on our land?'

Innis stifled a laugh. It wasn't their land, not yet.

'We're just doing our job, miss,' said the second man.

'What is this thing?' Innis asked, pointing to the device that sat on top of the tripod. It looked like a cross between a speed camera and a Star Wars droid.

'It's called a theodolite,' said the man standing closest to it. 'It's an instrument for measuring angles in the horizontal and vertical planes. I can show you how it works if you like.'

Innis waved away the request. 'No, that's okay.' He could imagine nothing worse than knowing how a theodolite worked.

Kat peered through the viewfinder. 'So, has it told you how many?'

'How many what?' asked the man.

'How many wind turbines you can fit across the Barrens?'

A glance of panic shot between the two surveyors.

'Oh, relax,' Kat said, 'My dad works for the council. I know all about your plans.'

'We're just surveying the land,' said one of the men.

'Well this land doesn't need wind turbines. Can't you put them offshore?'

'That's a more expensive option.'

'But it is possible?'

'We don't make those decisions.'

'Then we're talking to the wrong people.'

Kat pulled on Innis's arm and they moved away, back towards the crofts.

'That was a bit rude,' Innis said.

'We're not here to make pals. The turbines can go elsewhere, that man said so. We have to show them that the Barrens is the wrong choice.'

'And how do you intend to do that?'

'I don't know exactly. But that's Plan A.'

'And what's Plan B?'

She stopped and gave him a serious look. 'I suppose it will have to be your leap.'

'But you said my leap was stupid.'

'It is. Very stupid. That's why it's Plan B. Better to convince the people who are building the turbines that the Barrens isn't the place for them.'

'I'm not sure they'll listen.'

'If we tell them about our dark skies, how they have to be preserved, how we are about to become an International Dark Sky Community. If we tell them that, they'll *have* to listen.'

Innis didn't understand big business for a minute, but he was certain they wouldn't care much about a bunch of island stargazers.

'Just be careful, Kat,' he said. 'This is some giant energy company you're up against.' He gave her a sympathetically cheeky smile. 'Your charm and good looks will only get you so far.'

'I shall rely more on my steadfastness and above-average intelligence.'

'Then we'll have to call you *Hermione* McColl.'

Kat smiled and punched him on the arm. They were friends again.

Chapter 19

A wet wind was blowing in off the sea on Monday afternoon as Innis made the short walk from school to the hostel. He was looking at his phone, smiling as he strolled. Kat had just sent him a message and he could tell she was excited. He could judge her level of excitement by the numbers of emoji attached to the end. This was a twelve-emoji spectacular. She had just received an email from America – Nin was about to be accepted as an International Dark Sky Community. She had finished her message with the words, *The turbines have to be stopped!*

Innis closed the app and opened the webpage he had been looking at earlier. Kat's Plan A was already up and running. Overnight, she had founded a protest group to save the Barrens. She had even come up with a catchy name for the organization.

The Guardians of Nin.

Innis had laughed when he first saw the webpage, but then felt bad. This was exactly what he was trying to be with his leap: a guardian of the island.

As he walked his eyes were focused on his phone. He jolted in fright when a figure emerged from the shadow of a wall by the seafront.

'Hello again,' the man said.

It was the man from the ferry ramp, the one with the website. His long hair was tied in a ponytail now, and his beard seemed a little tidier.

'What do you want?' Innis said, judging the distance from where he stood to the hostel front door. He could see light spilling from the windows of the building.

'Five minutes of your time, that's all.'

'If I screamed they would hear me from the hostel.'

'Why would you scream?'

'If you attacked me.'

The man laughed. 'Why would I attack you?'

'I don't know. You seem to be following me.'

'I'm not following you. I'm trying to talk to you. If I was following you I would have come to Nin.'

'Have you waited here all weekend?'

'I've been working. You're not my only contact on the island. There's a guy who's going to climb the Old Man of Storr without a safety rope.'

The Old Man of Storr was a famous pinnacle of rock jutting from a peninsula of Skye.

'Well, that's just daft,' Innis said.

'No more daft than leaping a large gap in a cliff face.'

Was that a compliment or a criticism? Innis wondered. 'And what do you do?'

'I film the attempt and stream it live on my website.'

'For people to watch?'

'If you subscribe to the website you get instant access to all manner of stunts and deeds of daring.'

Innis snorted. 'People pay to watch someone fall to their death?'

'People pay to watch someone make it successfully to the top.'

'With a good chance that they will fall to their death.'

'That's the excitement of it.'

'What do you call your website again?'

The man moved forward and offered Innis a business card. 'Aff yer heid dot com.'

'I think you'd have to be.'

'Oh, let's not be snobby about it. You'll see the same on YouTube. We just offer an *as it's happening* experience. Live chats, comments, real-time tweets. All as you watch.'

Innis read the business card. 'Matt McGowan.'

'That's me. When are you doing your leap?'

'I haven't decided yet. We have our two-week Easter holiday coming up. I thought sometime then.'

'Well, I think your leap would be perfect for the website. We would do loads of pre-publicity, you would be all over social media. Then we would stream the leap live on the day. You would get a fee up front to begin with and then a percentage of the income generated from subscriptions and downloads.'

'And what happens if I don't make it?'

'You nominate a beneficiary in the unlikely event that something goes wrong.'

Matt McGowan sounded sincere, but Innis knew that 'something going wrong' was the reason people subscribed.

'Can you imagine,' the man continued, 'the whole world watching you do your leap? Australians and Americans and Chinese, all cheering on the boy from the small Scottish island. And when you land on the other side the world will shout in triumph; planet Earth will do a collective fist bump for the new Laird of Nin.'

Matt McGowan was laying it on thick, but there *was* something exciting about the thought. If he was going to do the leap anyway, why not have the world watching on?

'Think about it tonight,' the man said. 'I'll come round with a contract tomorrow. You can sign it or not. Whatever you think.'

'Doesn't an adult need to sign it?'

Matt McGowan gave an awkward shrug. 'It's more of a disclaimer than a contract. Just to keep everything right and proper. It *will* guarantee you a fee, however.'

'Okay,' Innis said hesitantly. 'I'll think about it.'

Chapter 20

When Innis entered the head teacher's office on Thursday morning, two things instantly caught him by surprise. Firstly, Kat was sitting there. Kat was only summoned to Mr MacDonald's office to receive academic awards. Innis could tell from the head teacher's grim face that there were no prizes being handed out this morning.

The second surprise came at the sight of a policeman standing in the room. He held his cap in his hands and the radio perched on his shoulder crackled quietly.

'Sit down, Mr Munro, please,' said the head teacher.

There were now two plastic chairs in front of his desk. Innis moved to the empty one, shooting a glance in Kat's direction. She looked mortified that she should be here, sitting on the bad boys' seat.

The policeman stepped to the centre of the room and laid his cap on the desk.

'Don't worry folks, you're not in trouble,' he said. 'This concerns your home island of Nin. That's why I'm talking to you both.'

Panic gripped Innis. Was the policeman here to ban the leap?

The sergeant paced slowly in front of them. 'Now I know you are aware of the plans to build wind turbines on Nin.'

'What makes you think that?' Kat asked.

The policeman gave the girl a bemused smile. 'You have a website. It's a protest group to stop the turbines.'

'Of course,' she said quietly.

'Unfortunately, the company who are building the turbines have had some problems on the island this week. Damage to their equipment, things going missing, that kind of thing.'

'And you think we did it?' Kat asked.

'No, not at all,' the policeman said. 'In fact, I know you didn't. The vandalism began on Monday and you were both at school. You've been in school all week. It's someone else who's causing the trouble.'

'So why are we here?' Kat asked.

'I'm just checking to see if you've heard anything that might help my enquiries.'

'Nothing,' the girl said firmly.

Innis sensed heads swivel in his direction, although

he was staring at the floor. He was just relieved that the leap was not being banned. 'I know nothing either.'

'Employees of the company mentioned that they had talked to you both last weekend.'

'They were surveying the Barrens,' Kat said. 'They showed us one of their instruments.'

'And do you remember which instrument that was?'

Innis did remember. 'It was called a theodolite.'

The policeman nodded. 'Aye. That's one of the things that has gone missing.'

'Why would someone take a theodolite?' Innis asked.

'To stop the surveying. To disrupt the turbines being built.' The sergeant turned his attention to Kat. 'On your Twitter page, you encourage those of a like mind to –' he flicked open his police notebook – '"disrupt and delay by whatever means possible". What exactly did you intend by that statement?'

Kat slid down on her seat. 'I just meant by marches and petitions. I didn't encourage stealing stuff.'

'And do you know of someone who might have taken it in a way you didn't intend?'

'Last time I checked, my tweets only had one follower.'

'That would be me,' Innis offered.

'You have more followers now,' said the policeman. 'And one of them, perhaps, has taken things a wee bit too far.'

'Well I don't know who,' Kat said softly.

Innis looked at her face, saw her chew her lip the way she always did when she told a lie.

'Okay.' The policeman shut his notebook and lifted his hat from the desk. 'If either of you hear anything or suspect anything it is important that you tell us.'

'Do you understand what the sergeant is asking?' said Mr MacDonald gruffly.

'Aye,' Kat said. Innis nodded.

The head teacher flicked his hand to indicate that Innis and Kat were to remove themselves. They retreated from the office in silence and moved along the corridor in the same manner, not speaking until they were well out of sight of Mr MacDonald.

'Oh God,' Kat said.

'Aye, it's a bit much, accusing us just because we're from Nin.'

'It's not that. I never got the chance to tell you earlier. Lachlan is missing.'

'*Missing?* In what way?'

'Missing, as in, no one's sure where he is.'

'He'll be hiding in that abandoned dumpster he calls a caravan.'

'He's not, they've checked.'

She tugged him on the arm, dragging him into a quiet corner.

'His guidance teacher came to talk to me yesterday. Someone told her that Lachlan and I were friends. Lachlan hasn't been in school all week.'

'I was wondering where he was. You think he's back on Nin?'

'I don't know. The school phoned his uncle Dougal. He's listed as the emergency contact. Apparently, his uncle said he was back on the mainland with his parents. I doubt that. The school can't get a hold of his parents to confirm.'

'Have *you* tried calling him?'

'It goes straight to voicemail.'

'Text him.'

'I have done. Several times. I've had one reply.'

Kat held up her phone and allowed Innis to read the message. It was short and very much to the point.

Don't try and find me. Ever.

'Well, at least he's not dead.' Innis added with a smile, 'But you know what that proves?'

'It might not be him. He might be on the mainland.'

'No, of course it's him. Someone is skulking around Nin destroying things. Lachlan lives on Nin. Lachlan is missing. Lachlan sends you a text saying, "Don't try and find me. *Ever*." It is definitely, absolutely, positively, Lachlan Geddes.'

'I think you could have stopped at definitely.' Kat sighed. 'But why?'

'The energy company is trying to evict him from his croft and close the wildlife sanctuary. That's reason enough.'

'But why doesn't the school suspect it's Lachlan? He's

been gone four days. Why are the police not looking for him?'

'Maybe they are.' Innis thought about it for a moment. 'Or, maybe the school has no idea that Lachlan has any connection with Nin. Remember, his address is listed as that silly wee caravan. How would the school know he goes back to the island at weekends?'

'But his uncle is from Nin.'

'His uncle is just an emergency contact. His parents live on the mainland. What do you know about them?'

'Not much. He's mentioned them, but he's quite secretive about it. There's something he's not telling me.'

'I wonder what else he's done.'

'I don't want to know.'

'I bet he's set his wolves on someone.'

'Enough with the wolves.'

Innis laughed, but suddenly it was clear. 'That's it. Lachlan has set the wolves free to try and scare the wind turbine people.'

'Oh, that's just silly. People would report it if they were chased by a wolf.'

'No one would believe them, that's the beauty of it. You didn't believe me that first night. You still don't. If people are too scared to come on to the Barrens because of the wolves the wind turbines will go elsewhere. It's only a matter of time before those surveyors get the fright of their lives.'

Kat sighed in despair. 'Well, if that's Plan C it's not

any better than Plan B.'

'We won't know anything until we're back on Nin.'

The girl nodded and looked around, but all was quiet. 'We better get back to class.'

'Or what?'

'Or we might miss something important.'

'Tomorrow is the last day before the holidays. No one is doing any work.'

'Maybe not in your classes.'

Ouch, Innis thought. There had been a time when he and Kat were together in every class.

'So, what are your plans for the holidays?' he asked, wanting to delay their return as long as possible.

'Nothing much. You'll be leaping to your death, I suppose.'

'I'll fit in my death leap at some point, I'm sure.'

Kat gave him a sad smile. She took out her phone and swiped a few times then handed it to Innis. 'I found this for you.'

He looked at the phone, watched the first few seconds of an athlete moving through the air in slow motion.

'It's a video that shows you how to do a long jump,' Kat said. 'If you eventually have to attempt this leap it would be good if you had the right technique. I'll send you the link.'

'Thanks. I'm sure it'll help.'

'It's still Plan B, remember. We focus our efforts on

protests and petitions.'

'We wouldn't have to bother with all that if I did the leap. I would own the Barrens.'

'Your leap is too dangerous. That's the last resort if nothing else has worked. It can wait.'

Innis handed back her phone. 'I'm still going to start training.'

He didn't want to tell her that he had signed a contract two days earlier. A date had already been set for the leap. It was the end of next week.

'I meant to say thanks,' she said.

'For what?'

'Your contribution to the Guardians of Nin fundraising. Every little helps. You've given ten pounds and my mum has given fifty.'

It took Innis a moment to do the sum. 'How many badges can you make with sixty pounds?'

'Well, here's the news. I checked this morning and we've had a third donation. An anonymous one. A donation of five hundred pounds.'

'That's a lot of badges.'

'I know. We can get proper posters made up, print flyers, make T-shirts, a whole bunch of stuff.'

'Who gave the money?'

'I haven't a clue, but it must be someone who really loves the Barrens.'

'Maybe it was Lachlan.' He added with a smile, 'How much does a theodolite cost on eBay?'

'Don't say that. Lachlan wouldn't do such a thing.'

Innis heard the uncertainty in her voice. Neither of them were certain exactly what Lachlan Geddes might do. Innis knew, however, that the donation hadn't come from stolen surveying equipment.

Tomorrow he would be back on Nin, back to the small island with the large cleft in its edge. A chasm he would have to leap across in a week's time. A leap which would be streamed live on the internet for all to witness. To see him either land or plunge.

A spectacle for which he had been paid £500.

Chapter 21

Innis had been on the moor all morning, practising his long jump technique. A deal had been made with Matt McGowan. The leap was on. This was Plan A now, at least in Innis's head. This was the best way to save the Barrens.

He stood at the start of the flat piece of ground he was using as a practice run. He had watched the video Kat had found, and a few others. There were four key components to the long jump: the approach run, take-off, action in the air and landing. The landing was the least important bit. He wasn't trying to set a world record, he just wanted to get to the other side. A faceplant would do if it was on solid ground across the gap.

The approach run was supposed to be a gradual acceleration to the maximum speed possible. For a successful take-off, his last stride had to place his foot flat on the ground with his torso upright and his hips moving forwards. The action in the air could be either hang, sail or hitch-kick. Innis couldn't remember which one was which, thought he would hope simply for a strong wind at his back. By that point there wouldn't be much he could do anyway.

Innis took off running, sprinting as hard as he could. He had marked a run-up with a hollow at the end. He reached the spot where the ground sloped away and launched himself. He soared across the dip with ease and landed on the moorland, tumbling over as he fell forwards.

He picked himself up and brushed himself down. That had been easy, a two-metre leap already. He looked to the sky; there was a scattering of clouds but the sun was trying to give warmth to the land. He had trained enough for one day. There was probably no need to train again. He could jump two metres. All he required now was the courage to do it over a deep drop down to certain death. He looked across the Barrens. Lost Lachlan and his wolves were out there somewhere. He was sure of it.

Innis started walking across the rough ground, stepping from hummock to hummock, avoiding the small pools of dark water. He was heading for *Beinn Ainmhidhean* in the far distance, the Hill of the Beasts. It seemed an appropriate name now. That was where the wolves seemed to gather. Innis was certain if he found the animals again he would find Lachlan. He wanted to know if it was Lachlan doing the vandalism. The damage was small-scale – tyres being deflated, equipment being taken apart – but he'd heard it being called *acts of sabotage*.

There was no sign of human life, he had the Barrens to himself again, just the way he liked it. Innis walked unhurriedly towards the mountain. To his right, something caught his eye. It stood above the ground, yellow in colour, but it wasn't gorse. He walked closer and saw it was a theodolite, standing on a tripod. Innis peered around in all directions. There was no one to be seen, just the abandoned instrument. A feeling of unease came upon him and he pulled his hood up and crept closer. Who had left it here, and why? When he reached the theodolite he peered through the viewfinder but could see nothing.

'Right you!' came a cry.

Innis whirled around and saw two men emerge from a hole, pushing back camouflage netting. It was a trap.

'Stay where you are!' shouted one of the men.

It took Innis just a second to assess the situation and make a decision. The two men were big, and dressed in some kind of camouflage clothing. They had been hiding and watching, waiting for someone to approach the theodolite. They were goons of the energy company, expecting some act of vandalism, but he had done nothing wrong.

In that brief moment, Innis considered doing as instructed and staying where he was, arguing his case of mistaken identity. Then he thought about the questions that would follow: Who are you? Why are you here? What are you doing? He wanted to talk to Lachlan before he landed him in it. Innis turned and ran.

'Oi! You!' came a voice from behind him.

Innis glanced back, saw the two men following. The chase was on.

This was not the first time he had run across the Barrens and his footing was sound. He could distinguish instinctively the firm ground from the marsh. He leapt from hummock to hummock, heard the men cursing and splashing behind him. He shot a glance backwards and saw one of the big, heavy bodies sink into a swampy hollow. He was putting distance between them. Then he was on flatter, drier ground. He urged his legs on, could feel his lungs burning.

Ahead he saw a pickup truck drive up the track by his croft. The truck had the distinctive logo of the energy company on its doors. The chasing heavies had called for backup.

Innis changed direction, heading east towards the sea. He had a stitch in his side and his options were narrowing by the second. Behind him were the two bruisers, to the south was the pickup, in front was only cliff edge. He veered north, unsure where he was heading but sensing the net closing in. He could see the ruin of Nin

Castle ahead. If he could reach the crumbling walls he might find a hiding spot inside. He increased his pace, but when he looked again another two men were moving from the castle in his direction. It was an elaborate trap to catch the island saboteur.

Innis slowed to a stop and stood panting with his hands on his knees. There was nowhere left to go. He straightened up and stood looking out to sea. The ocean sparkled in the sunshine and on the far horizon he could see the Scottish mainland.

Something broke cover beside him. It was the big black wolf, leaping from a bush. It headed straight for him, teeth bared, and for a terrifying moment Innis thought it was pouncing. Instead the animal bounded past and headed towards the cliff edge. Innis gasped as he watched it hurtle towards the drop. The wolf reached the edge and stopped. It turned and looked at him then disappeared over the cliff.

Innis gasped again. *The wolf had gone over the cliff.* He ran towards the spot and peered cautiously over the drop. There was no sign of a dead wolf on the beach below. The surf was gently rolling up the sand undisturbed. Just below his feet he noticed a ledge of stone. He looked to the left and saw the ledge move down and along the cliff face. At first glance it looked like the curve of the rock but from this spot, where it began, he could see it was a path of sorts, narrow and precipitous but seeming to lead somewhere. Had the wolf jumped down on to the ledge and escaped? Could he do the same?

Innis looked around him and noticed that here at the cliff edge the ground dipped down. The chasing men couldn't see him from this position. They wouldn't have seen the wolf either. He crouched down and peered over the drop. The ledge was right below him, but so was a long plunge to the beach below. There was no time for fear. He swung himself around and lowered himself on to the ledge, his fingers grasping the top of the cliff. He fixed his gaze on the rock face in front of him and tried to slow his breathing. Now that he was standing on the stone platform he realized it was wide enough to walk two abreast, but still he pressed himself hard against the cliff, away from the edge of the ledge.

What now? He could wait here and hope the men gave up the chase, but all it would take was a curious peek over the cliff edge and he would be discovered. The wolf had disappeared, so it must have followed the ledge to somewhere. The cliff curved as it stretched away from him so he couldn't see where the path led, only that it headed downwards. Perhaps he could follow it all the way to the beach?

Innis began moving along the ledge, hugging the wall and not looking down. His fear of heights made his legs shake but he knew this was the kind of bravery he would have to muster on the day of the leap. He kept moving, forcing one foot in front of the other. He had the sudden, anxious thought that if the ledge just came to an abrupt end, he would meet an angry wolf there and have nowhere to go.

Innis moved around the curve of the cliff and saw that the rock face was no longer smooth. Ahead, the cliff seemed fractured and jagged, and Innis doubted the path could stretch much further. He moved on anyway. The ledge began to narrow and he feared the worst. He took a glance to his right and saw only the surge of waves far beneath him spilling up the beach. He was halfway down the cliff face now but it was still a deadly drop to the bottom.

He pressed on a few more steps, saw the ledge disappear into the rock face. The end, perhaps in more ways than one. He pushed his back against the cliff face, moved a couple of more paces and then with a suddenness that made him scream, he found himself falling.

Not from the cliff face though. He had fallen the other way, through a hole in the rock. Innis lifted himself to his feet, his heart thumping hard, and saw that he was in a cave. The ledge path led to a cave in the cliff. The opening was narrow and the inside seemed deep and dark. Innis stepped inside. The air was cool and he heard his sharp breaths echo off hidden walls.

A secret cave. He felt a quick flash of excitement, and at that same moment he heard a low growl.

Innis caught his breath, felt an ancient dread course through his body like electricity. He stood frozen and as his eyes adjusted to the dark he could make out the silhouette of the wolf. It stood erect, its head pointing in his direction, its sharp white teeth catching the meagre light from the faraway hole. For a moment that felt like a lifetime, boy and beast stared at one another. Then Innis took a step back, resisting the urge to flee in terror, fighting to keep his movements unhurried and calm. *I will turn and walk slowly from this cave*, he told himself.

Innis turned and looked and whimpered. At the mouth of the cave another animal stood, barring his way. To his left and right were the outlines of other beasts.

He was trapped in a den of wolves.

Chapter 22

Innis couldn't tell how many wolves surrounded him. He could hear snuffling and low growls in the dark, and at least one animal was pacing. It seemed only a matter of time before he was devoured. He stood trembling for a long minute and wished they would just get on with it.

Nothing happened. The wolves seemed wary. The big one stepped towards him slowly, bowed its head slightly and sniffed. There was no aggression from it, the wolf seemed only . . . curious.

A noise echoed in the cave, like a footstep on stone, and then a voice. A human voice. A human voice in this den of wolves.

'Innis, you idiot.'

He turned and saw a sight so unreal that he didn't

trust his eyes. It looked like Lachlan Geddes over by the wall, floating above him in the dark.

'Move this way, slowly,' said the voice in whisper.

Innis obeyed, walked painstakingly towards the apparition. He moved past the wolf, which turned its head to watch him go. As he got closer he saw that it was indeed Lachlan Geddes. He wasn't floating – he stood in the entrance to a passageway that was raised above the ground. Lachlan reached down and Innis took his hand and allowed himself to be hauled up from the cave floor. His feet scrambled on the wall for purchase and he fell through the opening. He knelt there for a few moments, felt his heart hammer in his chest like his ribs might break. He looked up. Lachlan was staring as if it was him, not Innis, who had seen a ghost.

'Follow me,' the boy said.

Innis followed behind and after a few metres the corridor led to a set of stone steps. Lachlan was using the light on his phone to illuminate the way. They moved up the stone stair, their footsteps echoing around the narrow passageway.

'What is this place?' Innis asked. He had lost count of how many steps he had climbed.

'Just keep moving.'

The staircase led to another passageway which ended in a wall of rock. They walked along it to the end. Lachlan handed his phone to Innis then reached up and pushed. The ceiling lifted up with a creak. It was a trapdoor.

Lachlan pushed it all the way open then took back his phone, switching off the torch. A weak light spilled in from above.

'What is this place?' Innis asked again.

'You'll see.'

Lachlan grabbed hold of the side of the opening and pulled himself out. He reached down and again helped Innis up. He closed the trapdoor behind him and kicked rubble over the top, disguising the entranceway.

Innis looked around him. He was in another narrow passageway, but this one had walls of crumbling stone that stretched high above and there was no roof at the top.

'This is the castle,' Innis said.

'Aye, it is.'

Innis shook his head in amazement. 'And that's a secret passageway.'

'And I'm sure there's many more in this old place, but that's the only one I know of.'

Innis had a million questions to ask but Lachlan had a finger to his lips. He motioned for Innis to stay where he was as he disappeared down the passageway. Innis stood in the half-light and tried to control his breathing, tried to slow his heart rate. A few minutes earlier he had stood among wolves. Looking back, the animals had seemed almost friendly. Lachlan returned.

'The wolves are real,' Innis said. 'You can't deny it now.'

After a pause, Lachlan replied, 'Aye, maybe so.'

'Why didn't they attack me?'

'I don't know. That was bizarre. That behaviour is new. I haven't seen that many together in the cave before.' The boy looked around him anxiously. 'But we need to get out of here. The men seem to have gone for now.'

'They'd set a trap.'

'I watched you climb down on to the ledge. Why were they chasing you?'

Innis gave Lachlan a puzzled frown. 'They thought I was you. It's you they're looking for.'

'Because I've skipped school for a few days?'

'No! Because of the sabotage that's been going on.'

'What *sabotage*?' The boy said sabotage as if it was the strangest of word choices.

Innis gave a look of disbelief. 'Someone's been damaging the energy company's equipment. The police were at school.'

Lachlan shook his head. 'It's nothing to do with me.'

'It *has* to be you. They're trying to evict you.'

'That won't happen. You've got it all wrong.'

'But it has to be you. Kat thinks so as well.'

'Well it isn't me. And tell Kat to stop texting. I'll be back when I'm ready to come back.'

Lachlan disappeared down the castle corridor. Once again, the boy had saved the day and then made it difficult to be grateful. Innis moved after him, stepping over the rubble that lay across the floor. He caught glimpses of dark doorways and dim alcoves and wondered how Lachlan knew about the secret passageway he had just climbed through. The boy had not been long on the island.

Lachlan stood at the castle doorway with his jacket in his hands. It was a thick Puffa coat, black with an orange lining.

'Here, swap,' he said.

'Why?'

'Because those men are heading in the direction of your croft. I assume you want to go home sometime. If you keep that hoodie on they'll know it was you that ran. Did they get a look at your face?'

'I don't think so, my hood was up. But I haven't done anything.'

'That makes two of us. But you'll spend hours in a room somewhere trying to convince them of that.'

Innis took off his hoodie and handed it to Lachlan. He put on Lachlan's jacket, which was a little short in the sleeves.

'When you reach the men, try to draw their attention up here,' Lachlan said.

'Why?'

'Just do it.'

'Why are you helping me like this? I thought you *didn't do nice*.'

'I don't. But there's something strange going on between you and the wolves and I need to find out what.'

'I'm not tracking them. They're coming to me.'

'Exactly.'

Lachlan was unwilling to say more but at least now he had acknowledged the wolves' existence. Innis left the castle and tried to stride with a confident air along the cliff edge and then down the hill towards the crofts. The men from the company, five of them in total, were in a tight huddle but separated when they saw him approach. Innis hoped again that none of them had seen his face.

'You there,' one of the big men said, 'what are you doing out here?'

Innis pointed to the crofts a little further along the track. 'I live here.'

'But what are you doing?'

Innis said it again with emphasis. 'I *live* here.'

'Are you trying to be cheeky, mate?' said the big man.

A familiar voice interjected, saving Innis from having to respond.

'Can I help you gentlemen with something?' It was Gramps.

'This little tyke isn't answering my question.'

Innis's grandfather walked slowly up to the man. 'This little tyke happens to be my grandson. And unless you're a police officer, and I know for a fact that you are not, I don't believe he is under any obligation to answer anything you ask. Now, assuming you don't want to face the serious accusation of harassing a child, I suggest you move away from here and don't go near my grandson again.'

'Easy, old fellow,' the man said. 'We're just looking for

the person responsible for the vandalism. I'm sure you've heard about it.'

'I have, aye, and it's got nothing to do with us.'

'We were chasing someone earlier. He looked a bit like your grandson.'

Gramps had steel in his voice when he said, 'Well, it wasnae him.'

Innis remembered Lachlan's instruction and looked back towards the Barrens. There was Lachlan in the far distance, wearing the hoodie, waving.

'There's someone over there,' Innis said, with a nonchalant point of the finger. 'Is that who you were chasing?'

The second big man cursed and took a step in Lachlan's direction but he was halted by a grab of his arm.

'Leave it,' said the first man. 'We'll never catch him now. Next time.'

'We'll be getting back home, then,' said Gramps.

The man sighed. 'Yeah, sorry to trouble you. Sorry, mate.'

Innis gave a dismissive shake of the head and helped his grandfather back in the direction of their croft. He wondered if Gramps had noticed the jacket change. Halfway down the road he heard loud swearing from one of the men. He turned to look. They were all crowded round the truck, staring at the front tyres.

'I think they've lost the air in their tyres again.'

His grandfather gave a quiet chuckle and Innis knew

Lachlan had been lying. Lachlan *was* the saboteur.

Back at the croft, Innis settled his grandfather into his chair with a hot drink. He had loved the way Gramps had come to his defence, no questions asked. He would do whatever it took to make sure his grandfather was comfortable in his last years of life, and that meant ensuring he could stay here in the croft. And that meant being Laird of Nin. And *that* meant jumping successfully from one side of the leap to the other.

Once Gramps was snoozing in front of the fire, Innis went outside. He looked towards the coast, smiled at the thought that not too far away there was a cave in which wolves gathered. He hung Lachlan's jacket on the washing pole.

In the morning it was gone, replaced by his hoodie.

Chapter 23

Innis had been desperate to see Kat all day but knew he would have to wait until Sunday service was finished. It was just after lunch when he pushed open the back door of her croft and entered the kitchen. He was family, he didn't have to knock.

Kat was sitting at the kitchen table, a pile of books almost obscuring her face. She didn't do homework in her bedroom where there were too many digital distractions.

'We're on holiday for two weeks,' Innis said. 'Why are you doing school work?'

Kat didn't look up from her study of the equal and opposite forces of Newton's third law of motion. 'Without exercise your brain gets flabby, just like every other bit of your body.' She was way ahead of the rest of her Physics class, but if she was to be an astronomer and astronaut she had to put in the extra hours.

Innis moved into the room and sat in the armchair by the fireplace.

'I saw Lachlan yesterday.'

'Oh aye,' the girl said.

'Out on the Barrens.'

She made a few notes in her jotter, then asked without looking up, 'And how is he?'

'He seems okay. Says it's not him doing the sabotage. I don't believe him. He had a message for you.'

'Oh aye,' she said again.

Innis tried not to sound too smug. 'He asked you not to text him any more.'

The girl flicked to the next page in her textbook. 'Oh, I gave that up days ago.'

'He says he'll come back when he's ready and not before.'

'Good for him,' she said coldly. After a moment she asked, 'So where's he been hiding?'

'I'm not really sure. The castle I think. Or there's a cave, but that's full of wolves.'

Kat gave a mocking snort. He was going to argue but there seemed little point. Until the girl saw the wolves with her own eyes she would never believe him.

'I saw that website,' she said after a moment of silence.

'It's just announced the date for your leap. Saturday coming.'

'That's right.'

'You're actually going ahead with it?'

'I am. I've got a week to practise but I don't really need it.'

'Oh God, Innis,' she said quietly. 'You're going to die.'

'How many times? It's not that far.'

Kat tapped her textbook as if it contained the secrets of the universe. 'That just accounts for your horizontal motion. In calculating the distance to travel you also have to consider vertical motion. You'll accelerate downward due to the gravitational pull of the Earth. To compensate for this, you'll need to acquire sufficient height on your take-off. You need height. And – trust me when I say this Innis – you can't fly!'

Innis hadn't understood a word of Kat's science lecture. 'Well *you* can't tell a rook from a raven but you don't hear me complain.'

Kat sighed and shook her head. 'The leap was supposed to be Plan B. You weren't meant to actually do it. We can save Nin's dark skies by protesting and persuading. Plan A, remember? Convince the energy company to put the turbines offshore and not on the Barrens.'

Innis stared at the fire flickering in the hearth and knew he could never explain to Kat the different reasons he wanted to leap. It wasn't just about saving the Barrens.

It was also about stopping Gramps being shipped to the mainland. And it was about him, Innis Munro, the unexceptional boy from the small island, doing something remarkable. Something incredible. Something that had never been done before. The leap was him making a mark on a world that up to this point hadn't really noticed he was there.

'Can't we do both?' he asked.

'Not if one involves you plummeting to your death.'

'Well, I can't back out now. I've been paid money by the website that's going to stream the leap.'

'Give the money back.'

'I don't have it any more.'

'Did you spend it already?'

'No, not exactly. I didn't spend it, I gave it away.'

'Gave it away to . . .' Kat's words faded slowly as the realization hit home. 'Oh Innis, you didn't?'

'It was a good cause. I thought it would get your campaign started.'

'But I've spent most of it on posters and T-shirts and banners.'

'Good. I don't want it back. It's done now.'

The girl had a panicked look on her face. 'You are not leaping to your death because I've spent your money. I'll find the five hundred pounds from somewhere. I'll borrow it from my mum and dad if need be.'

Innis gave her a smile, grateful for her concern. 'I told you, I don't want it back. I'm going to do this leap and make it to the other side. It's only two metres. I don't need height. Not every bird needs to fly.'

Kat closed her eyes and bowed her head. 'Tell that to the dodo.'

Chapter 24

Early on Monday morning Innis and Kat walked down to Skulavaig. Kat had a large canvas bag over her shoulder full of posters protesting against the wind turbines. She had asked Innis to lend a hand, hoping it might help him accept Plan A and abandon Plan B.

'Where to first?' Innis asked.

'The cafe.'

They walked around the edge of the large, modern harbour, built to accommodate the ferries that sailed from Skye to Nin every day. The cafe had a view past the harbour and out over the ocean. Hence the name above the big window; *Cafe C the C*.

Innis and Kat went in, setting the bell above the door ringing. The place was empty; not quite morning coffee time yet. A small, round woman appeared from the back.

'Good morning, Katrina,' she said. 'What can I do for you?'

'Morning, Mrs Fitzpatrick. I was hoping you might put one of these up in your window.'

Kat pulled a poster from her bag and unrolled it, spreading it across one of the empty tables. It was glossily produced, with a picture of a wind turbine with a cross through it beneath bold words that said, SAVE THE BARRENS. At the bottom were details of the Guardians of Nin website.

Innis wondered how much support there would be among the townspeople. There were rumours of jobs coming to the island along with the turbines. The Barrens was a difficult place to get to, with nothing much of interest once you were there. Its emptiness and stillness was its beauty but that didn't fire people's imagination and get them out protesting.

'Nice posters,' he said.

'It's amazing what five hundred pounds can buy you,' Kat said with a frown.

'Let me hang it up here,' Mrs Fitzpatrick said, pointing to the wall by the door.

The poster was fixed for all to see, and as Innis and Kat were leaving, the cafe owner said, 'I hope your preparations are going well, Innis. We're all very proud of you here in Skulavaig.'

'Thanks,' Innis said awkwardly.

They left the cafe and walked up the road towards

the local convenience store.

Innis asked, 'How does she know about the leap?'

Kat scowled. 'Everyone knows about it. You should come into town more often.'

When they entered the little shop, the owner, a tall, thin man with white hair and white whiskers, came out from behind the counter.

'There's the boy himself,' the man said, 'Nin's very own celebrity.'

'Oh, I don't think so,' Innis said, embarrassed.

'Of course you are, look what arrived on the morning ferry.'

The man returned to his counter and lifted a newspaper from the top of a large pile. He handed it to Innis. It was this week's *Western Isles Gazette*. On the front were two short stories about the island of Nin. A single story about the island was unusual enough. Two stories on the front page had never happened before.

The first report was about the vandalism to equipment and vehicles of the wind turbine company. Innis glanced through the article and saw the words *unknown perpetrator* and *stepped up security*. He didn't read in-depth, however, as his interest was immediately focused on the other report. The obvious attention-grabber was the photograph of himself. It was the same picture that the young woman reporter had taken almost two weeks earlier. How long ago that seemed now. Back then he had only merited a mention on the newspaper website – now he was front-page news.

The article was short, with a brief description of the history of the leap, a few lines about Innis himself, some stuff about the internet interest that was being generated and an announcement of the date of the event.

'Oh God, Innis, you're on the front page,' Kat said. 'This thing is getting out of hand.'

Innis blew air out slowly through pursed lips. The unremarkable birdwatcher of the Barrens was on the front of the local newspaper. It gave him a tingly feeling to realize there was so much interest in him. Of course, if things went wrong it meant a lot more people would know about it. He would certainly be front-page news if the coastguard had to fish his dead body from the ocean.

'So, how's the training coming on, lad?' the shop-keeper asked.

'Fine,' Innis said. 'Just building up to the big day.'

'Tell me lad,' the man said with a wink, 'have you had a wee sneaky go already?'

'Don't encourage him!' Kat exclaimed. 'If he's sensible he won't even try.'

The old man waved away the notion. 'Of course he's doing it. Right lad?' The shopkeeper seemed to take Innis's silence as unspoken agreement. 'The whole of the island is rooting for you.'

They hung their poster and left the shop. Next they walked round to the Fishermen's Mission. This was a meeting place for some of the older islanders, a hall beneath the harbour master's office with a snooker table and dartboard and a crate full of empty whisky bottles. They pushed open the door and found the large room empty.

'We'll try later,' said Kat. She was halted by a voice from above. It was the harbour master coming down the stairs from his office.

'Miss McColl, how can I be of assistance?'

'Good morning, Mr Wallace,' Kat said. 'I was hoping you would put a poster in your window.'

She fetched a poster from her bag and showed it to him.

Mr Wallace straightened his blue harbour master's jacket and rubbed a hand across his trim beard. 'Ah yes, the Guardians of Nin. I thought that was my job.' He offered a half-smile, as if he was only half joking.

'We're trying to protect the Barrens from unwanted development. There are other places the wind turbines can go.'

'Aye, out at sea. Which will only make my job harder. I'm afraid I cannae hang your poster lass, as I cannae support your cause. There's nothing to see on the Barrens, a wind turbine or two willnae be a blight.'

'Fifty-eight, actually,' Innis said.

'It's more their location than their number. The ocean is my concern first and foremost. Inland will be yours to worry about.' The harbour master struck a conciliatory tone. 'But leave one and I'll see if the old boys will hang it up down here.'

'Thank you,' Kat said.

Mr Wallace turned to Innis. 'And you, lad.'

'Aye Mr Wallace?'

'If you're going to do this leap of yours, and naturally I wish you the best of luck, if you are going to do it, make sure it's on the other side of the island, away from my window.'

'Aye, Mr Wallace.'

Even the harbour master, a man of no small importance on Nin, knew and had an opinion on Innis's leap.

They left the mission and walked past the old harbour. A small lobster boat with a wooden wheelhouse was the only vessel on the water.

'Let's go round to the ferry,' Kat said.

They walked back to the big harbour but the ferry was still an hour from arriving. Kat went into the small ticket office to offer them a poster. Innis stayed by the pier. He was tired of hanging posters, though they had only done a few.

Kat came bursting out of the ticket office and beckoned Innis over. She didn't look happy.

'You better come and hear this,' she said to him.

Together they moved into the office. It was a cramped space with a counter on one side and two chairs and a stand full of tourism leaflets on the other. The man behind the counter was small and English.

'Tell him what you've just told me,' Kat said to him.

The man laughed. 'I was just telling Katrina about the impact your leap is having on ferry bookings. On the day of your leap the number of passengers booked on the early boat is three times more than normal.'

'Why?' Innis asked, not quite grasping what it all meant.

'They're coming to see you,' the man said.

'You're kidding?'

'The hotel is fully booked as well.'

Innis couldn't quite believe what he was hearing. This was just a silly notion of his. It had been the talk of the school for a while but that was all.

'But how do they know about it?' he asked.

'It's that website,' Kat said. 'You're trending. You've gone viral.'

'There's you and that other chap,' the ticket seller said, 'the one that's climbing the Old Man of Storr.'

'Without a rope, apparently,' Kat added. 'And there's also a boy from Barra. He's going to jump over one of the causeways on a motorbike.'

'How do you know all this?' Innis asked, bemused and slightly troubled.

'It's all there on aff yer heid dot com. There's the motorbike jump, the climb up the rock and your Bonnie Laddie's Leap. They're calling it the Graveheart tour. Nice name. Haven't you been following?'

Innis shook his head. He had only looked at the website once and hadn't liked what he saw. If it wasn't a total wipeout it was an epic fail, and the stunts seemed to be getting progressively more dangerous. People falling off skateboards just didn't cut it any more.

'It's not really my thing.'

'Well, it's proving very popular – now the whole world is going to watch you do your stupid leap.'

Innis gave a long, long sigh. This was what he had wanted, what he had been promised; a fame of sorts. But now that it was here the thought terrified him. He wasn't sure if he craved the whole world any more, and wondered if a bleak moorland on a small island might just be world enough.

'I need some air.'

He left the ticket office and stood by the harbour while Kat hung her poster. When she was done she came and stood next to him.

'Having second thoughts about your leap?'

Was he? Did he still want to be Lord of the Leap? Did he still want to be Laird of Nin?

Yes. *Yes!* More than ever. This was his destiny.

'No second thoughts. Of course I'm going to leap. You said it yourself, the world is watching. More than that. The world is coming!'

Chapter 25

Innis and Kat walked back up the road towards their crofts, enough posters hung for the day. On their right, the ocean had begun to roll in the growing wind. A wall of black cloud was approaching from the west. A storm was coming.

'We're about to get wet,' Innis said. Neither had brought a raincoat.

'My posters will be ruined,' groaned Kat, glancing at the posters sticking out the top of her bag.

They quickened their pace but knew the clouds were moving faster than their steps.

From the road ahead came a low growling sound. It got louder as it drew nearer and from around the bend appeared a quad bike. It was Lachlan. It seemed he was going to drive right by but he braked hard and pulled up beside them.

'All right?' the boy said awkwardly, addressing Kat. He didn't look glad to have been found.

'Where have you been all week?' she asked.

'Around.'

'You never texted me back.'

'My phone doesn't always get a signal.'

Innis knew the boy had got the texts just fine. 'Kat won't believe there's a cave full of wolves,' he said.

She would believe once Lachlan confirmed it.

'I have *no* idea what you're talking about,' Lachlan said.

'*What?*'

Innis took a step forward. Lachlan's muscles tensed and his hands made a fist. Kat stood between them.

'I think we should get moving,' she said. 'The storm's almost here.'

From the sky came a rumble of thunder, confirming her weather forecast.

'I'll give you a ride home on the quad if you like,' Lachlan said to Kat.

She looked hesitant for a moment. 'I suppose. I don't want my posters getting ruined.'

Lachlan unhooked a helmet from the back and handed it to Kat.

'Sorry,' he said to Innis, 'only one spare. Too dangerous to ride without a helmet.'

'Gramps didn't have a helmet.'

'We were going slowly then. Today we'll be just a bit faster.' He turned to Kat. 'You okay with faster?'

She nodded. 'Fast is good. One day I'll be strapped inside a rocket travelling at eighteen thousand miles per hour.'

Lachlan laughed. 'Well, I can't promise that speed, but hold tight anyway.'

He got back on the quad. Kat gave Innis an apologetic smile. She squeezed on her helmet and sat behind Lachlan.

'Don't get struck by lightning now,' the boy said with a grin, revving the engine.

'I didn't want to ride on the stupid thing anyway.'

Lachlan gunned the quad and the machine took off, leaving Innis in a roar of noise and cloud of exhaust smoke. The vehicle careered up the road and into the distance. Innis watched until it disappeared over a ridge. When he could no longer hear it, he began to walk.

The first drops began to fall a minute later and soon it was a downpour. Innis trudged through puddles in the road, water dripping from his face, waiting to be struck by lightning, uttering a curse with every step. He hated Lachlan Geddes, hated his smirk, hated his quad, hated his wolves. The boy had only just arrived on the island but roared around like he owned the place. Well, Innis would show him. He would cross the Bonnie Laddie's Leap in a single bound and then he *would* own the island. For real.

In the distance, he saw a glow of light through the dark of the storm. It was a car's headlights coming his way. As the car approached he stepped off the road to let it pass but instead the vehicle slowed. As it came to a stop he saw it was a police car.

The driver's window rolled down and the officer took a moment to look Innis up and down.

'Where are you off to, lad, in this weather?'

'I'm just heading home.'

'And where is home?'

'Not far. I live with my grandfather.'

There was a policewoman in the car as well, and the two officers gave each other a knowing look.

'What's your name?' the policewoman asked, leaning across.

'Innis. Innis Munro.'

'And where have you been today?'

He knew what was being implied. That he was up to no good. The police car was from Skye and the only reason it would be on Nin on a Monday afternoon was to keep an eye out for the island saboteur. And here he was, walking alone in the driving rain for no apparent purpose. Well, he wasn't going to be blamed for Lachlan Geddes's wrongdoing.

It was Lachlan roaming the island doing acts of petty vandalism, as if that would persuade anyone. It was Lachlan who didn't do nice, who had threatened to toss him off a cliff and tried to throw him off a boat. It was

Lachlan who had sped away on the quad and taken Kat with him.

'Why are you out here lad?' the policeman asked sternly.

Innis tried not to smile.

'I spotted the boy who's been doing the sabotage. He escaped on his quad bike.'

It was payback time.

'But I can tell you where he lives, if you like.'

Chapter 26

'Did you do this Innis?' Kat asked. 'To Lachlan?'

Innis stood in his dressing gown, newly awakened from a troubled sleep. 'He had it coming.'

'They've taken him to Skye this morning. Him and his uncle. In the back of a police car.'

'Really?' Innis gave an anxious puff of his cheeks. He hadn't expected the police to move so fast. Or so forcefully. He had expected a stern telling-off, nothing harsher.

'Why did you do it? He helped your grandfather down from the mountain.'

'Aye, but . . .'

Innis remembered how Lachlan had also helped three days earlier, when the goons were chasing. And how he had been happy to reveal the secret passageway in the cave. Those had been friendly acts. Was Lachlan Geddes a *friend*?

Innis took a sharp breath at the thought. Apart from Kat, he didn't really have any close friends. Had he given Lachlan enough of a chance? Was the boy only trying to protect his wolves? But if that was the case, why would he set them free? Their conversations had never been long enough or friendly enough for Innis to get to the truth.

'The police can't prove anything. He'll be fine.'

'For your sake, I hope so. If not you need to fix it.'

'Aye, okay.' Innis had no idea how to fix this one. It would take more than a jacket swap. He had landed Lachlan in it big time.

'So, what are you doing today?' he asked, changing the subject.

'Nothing much.'

Innis saw the twinkle. No one else could see the twinkle, but he could. Kat was up to something.

She turned for the door. 'I have to head up to the wildlife sanctuary for a wee bit. Lachlan sent me a text asking if I would unlock the wildcat house so they can get into their pen. He never had a chance to do it this morning.'

'You know how to do that?'

'He sent me instructions.'

'I'll come with you.'

'No,' she said, just a little too sharply. 'I'll go by myself. Lachlan might get back and he won't be happy to see you. He's worked out it must have been you who ratted on him.'

'Great.'

Kat departed and Innis made breakfast for him and Gramps. He lounged around the croft all morning and briefly thought about practising his leap, but it was in the bag already. If he practised too much he might get injured. That's what he told himself.

'Right lad,' said Gramps before lunch, 'we both need a bit of fresh air. Grab your coat.'

Innis groaned as he lifted himself from the armchair by the fire. It was the second day of the Easter break and he was now in holiday mode. It took an effort just to stand.

'Are you sure you're feeling well enough?'

'Fit as a fiddle,' Gramps said. 'Though dinnae ask me to dance to one.'

'Aye, no dancing. And no climbing mountains. Just a wee walk.'

Ten minutes later they were strolling along the coastal path towards the castle. The storm of the previous night had blown over and the air felt fresh under the warm sun. The ocean shimmered all the way to the mainland on the far horizon.

'Tell me lad,' Gramps said as he walked, 'have you seen those wolves again?'

The question caught Innis by surprise. It had been over a week since their climb up the mountain and

Gramps hadn't mentioned the wolves once since then. Innis had assumed his grandfather had forgotten.

Now was not the time to mention the wolf cave that lay beneath their feet. Gramps would want to go exploring. 'Maybe we just imagined them.'

His grandfather chuckled. 'They seemed real enough. There are quite a few island legends about wolves, you know.'

'I've heard one about Bonnie Prince Charlie.'

'Aye, that's a good one. The prince was fleeing from the English across the island and a pack of wolves helped him escape.'

'If you knew about that legend, why didn't you know about the leap?'

'I did lad, but I had forgotten all about it. It was years ago I last heard it mentioned. But all the old stories have been coming back to me.' He gave a sad smile. 'I think my brain is trying to remember everything one last time.'

They walked slowly on and Innis wondered why Gramps hadn't attempted the leap himself. How much easier it would have been if his grandfather was already Laird of Nin. No wind turbines then.

'There's another legend,' Gramps said, coming to a stop and looking out towards the ocean. 'The wolves helped the Bonnie Prince because they recognized the rightful King of Scotland. The legend states that the wolves could also recognize the Laird of Nin, and would honour him as well. Whenever a Laird died without a son and heir it was said the wolves picked the next Laird of the island.'

Innis felt a shiver run down his back as his grandfather continued.

'Of course, the wolves of Nin are as long gone as the Bonnie Prince, but maybe that's why old Geddes and his nephew brought the animals to our island. You cannae have a new Laird without some new wolves.'

'I don't think that's why Lachlan released the wolves.'

Gramps offered a mischievous grin. 'Maybe they werenae released. Maybe they just left. Maybe they came looking for you. After all, you are the next Laird of Nin, lad.'

Innis gave a doubting laugh. 'And how would the wolves know that?' But he had said as much to Lachlan himself; the wolves were coming to him.

He would have thought on it some more but his attention was grabbed by something drifting in the air. A burning smell.

'Something's burning.'

'Over there,' said Gramps.

Innis turned to look and could see a rising swirl of black smoke further up the path. The smoke was billowing around the tumbledown walls of Nin Castle.

'The castle's on fire!' he exclaimed.

'That cannae be good. Run lad, see what's happened. I'll catch you up.'

Innis ran along the path towards the castle. The

smoke was thick and black and gave off an unpleasant smell, like burning plastic. As he got closer he could see it was not the castle that was on fire. It was a vehicle. He slowed his run to walking pace. It was a pickup truck, and on the door he could still make out the logo of the energy company. It sat in front of the castle wall and was well alight now, flames rising from the back as if the pickup had been transporting fire. He could see that the cab in front was empty and he looked around, but there was no sign of anyone.

Innis edged closer, but not too close. He could feel the heat and hear hissing and popping noises along with the crackle of flame. He pulled his phone from his pocket and dialled 999. He gave details of the fire but knew it would be a while before anyone arrived to douse the flames. There was only a small fire engine in Skulavaig, manned by volunteer firefighters who would have to be contacted wherever they were on the island. Only then could they report to the fire station, don their firefighting gear and head for the fire. It was not a speedy process.

Innis moved back in case there was an explosion and sat on a low wall, watching the truck burn. He was joined eventually by his grandfather, who sat down beside him.

'Is there no one here?' Gramps asked.

'I can't see anyone. They would have come by now.'

'What set it ablaze?'

'I don't know.'

'I doubt the island saboteur would go this far.'

'It's a bit of a jump from letting air out of tyres to setting the whole truck on fire.'

Innis watched the paintwork of the door blister and knew it couldn't have been the work of Lachlan Geddes. Lachlan would still be on Skye. Lachlan couldn't be the saboteur. He had put the blame on an innocent person.

Now he really felt bad.

But if Lachlan wasn't the saboteur, who was? Was there someone else passionate enough about saving the Barrens that they would set fire to a pickup?

He could think of only one person.

Kat.

Could it have been Kat? Was she capable of this? Innis wasn't sure, but he thought it possible. He had seen the twinkle.

Whoever was responsible for the burning truck had taken the sabotage to a whole new level.

Now it was a crime.

Chapter 27

Innis needed to fix his mistake. Lachlan Geddes would be arriving on the afternoon ferry and the boy was due an apology. The thought of it was agonizing, but it had to be done.

The fire engine had come and doused the burnt-out truck. Still no one had come to claim it. Innis was back in the croft by the time a police car drove up the track for a look. He jumped on his bike and cycled south.

When he arrived at the harbour the ferry had just arrived, the ramp clanging on to the slipway. He parked his bike and saw Lachlan and his uncle Dougal emerge from the boat. He walked up to them, preparing himself for a headlock. Lachlan stopped and stood in silence.

His uncle moved away. 'I'll give you lads a minute.'

'I'm sorry,' Innis said.

'Why did you do it?'

'You rode off on your quad . . . with Kat . . . left me to walk home in the rain. I was annoyed and then the police car stopped. I didn't want them thinking the saboteur was me.'

Lachlan rubbed a hand across his shorn, fair hair. His dark eyes looked tired. 'Aye well, it wasn't me.'

'I know that now. There was more vandalism while you were on Skye.'

'So I heard.'

The two boys faced each other awkwardly for a moment before Innis said, 'I get it. I know the real reason why you're out on the Barrens. It's all about the wolves. You've had to release them because they're shutting down the wildlife sanctuary. Or maybe you're using the wolves to scare off the wind turbine people.'

Lachlan shook his head, seeming both amused and annoyed. 'Suppose you're right. How does it help if you post pictures and tell the world about our wolves? How does it help if you invite everyone to come and watch your leap right next to where I live? Why do you need an audience?'

'People are coming to see me leap, they're not coming to see your wolves.'

Lachlan laughed bitterly. 'I don't think you understand exactly what these people are coming to see.'

'They want to see me cross the Bonnie Laddie's Leap and claim the prize.'

Lachlan laughed again. 'If that's what you tell yourself.'

Innis knew exactly what Lachlan was implying. That people were coming to see him fall, not fly.

'Well maybe it's time the islanders knew that there are wolves on the Barrens. And the website filming my leap has thousands of followers. I'm sure a pack of wolves on the loose would get plenty of likes.'

For the first time, Lachlan showed a flicker of anger. 'Why would you do that?'

'I won't do anything if you just tell me the truth.'

Lachlan was in Innis's face now. 'The truth? You really want the truth? Well here it is. You couldn't jump the length of yourself. You will never make that leap. And then what? I'll tell you. You'll be dead and your doolally grandfather will be in a home for the deranged. That's the truth.'

Lachlan Geddes had gone too far. The boy could mock Innis all he wanted, put him in as many headlocks as he desired, feed him to the wolves if the fancy came, but Lachlan Geddes was never ever to speak ill of Gramps. Too far.

Innis launched himself at Lachlan and drove him on to the road, landing on top of the boy and grabbing his arms. Lachlan was powerful but Innis's strength was being fuelled by fury and he found himself straddling his opponent, pinning his arms to the ground. Lachlan struggled but he couldn't break free.

'Don't you ever speak about my grandfather that way, do you hear me?'

Lachlan writhed but Innis held tight. It felt fantastic to have the upper hand for once, but he couldn't keep Lachlan pinned to the ground for ever. In fact, his arms were beginning to wobble.

He was rescued by Lachlan's uncle, who grabbed him by the shoulders and hauled him up.

'Right, you two,' Uncle Dougal said, 'enough of that.'

Lachlan jumped to his feet and the man formed a barrier between the boys, both of them breathing hard and scowling harder.

Dougal Geddes chortled. 'I think you laddies have been needing to do that for a while.'

Lachlan looked at Innis and there was desperation in his eyes. 'You can't say a word about the wolves. If you do, everything my family have spent generations working for will be ruined.'

It was Innis's turn to snort. 'How can you ruin some rusty wire cages and a smelly old cowshed?'

'You don't understand. It's not the wildlife sanctuary that's important.'

'What then?'

For a moment, the only sound was the metallic clang of vehicles driving on to the ferry. The boys stared at each other with confused eyes.

'I think it's time you told him,' Dougal Geddes said.

Lachlan stood staring, breathing hard through his

nose, his mouth twitching.

'Tell me what?' Innis asked.

'We can't trust him,' Lachlan said.

'I think we can, lad. I think we have to.' There was silence for a moment more, and Lachlan looked unconvinced. Dougal Geddes added, 'I think he's the one.'

Lachlan looked Innis square in the eyes. 'Tomorrow morning. Meet me at the mountain. Seven o'clock sharp.'

'What for?'

'I'm going to show you something.'

'Show me what?'

Lachlan looked at his uncle, who nodded. 'Something that will change everything.'

Chapter 28

It was just before seven when Innis arrived at the mountain. The Barrens basked in the rising sunlight but the air was cold. Lachlan had told him not to be late and he had made a point of being early. Now he sat on a large rock and waited.

From far away he heard the growl of a quad bike engine and knew Lachlan was coming. Eventually he saw the boy and his machine speeding across the moor. When Lachlan arrived he left the engine running.

'Get on.'

Innis climbed on the back and asked, 'Where are we going?'

'You'll see.'

Lachlan gunned the quad and Innis grabbed the bar behind the seat. They drove past the big mountain, heading north towards a smaller group of hills. The ground sloped down, moorland turned to grass and they were off the Barrens.

This was a part of the island that Innis had never visited. His grandfather had always taken him to the mountain, because it was there that the eagles nested. Beyond were just some grassy hills with a few red grouse and rabbits.

At the bottom of what seemed the highest of the hills Lachlan stopped the quad. He climbed off, and said over his shoulder, 'Let's go.'

Innis looked up. The hill wasn't particularly high but the slope seemed almost vertical.

'We can't climb up there.'

'It's the quickest way.'

Lachlan began scrambling up the slope and Innis followed, bending his back and gripping the grass as he moved. He slipped a few times, thought he might slide back down to the bottom, but he kept climbing and made slow progress upwards. He pulled himself the last few metres on his hands and knees and crested the top.

Lachlan was lying flat on the ground, looking over. Innis joined him and peered down below. His eyes widened and his mouth fell open at what he saw there.

It was a small hidden valley. The ground was bounded on three sides by other hills and enclosed at the far end by a ridge of rocky moraine pushed there by a long-since melted glacier. A little stream ran down the gentle slope and at the bottom of the glen was a small but thick forest of birch trees, defiantly spreading stumpy branches towards the sun.

'Isn't it amazing,' Lachlan said in a whisper. 'There's barely an islander who knows this is even here. It's a little lost world on the edge of a bleak moor.'

'I had no idea,' Innis said.

He lay on his stomach, felt the morning sun on the back of his neck and listened to the gurgling of the small stream.

'There they are,' Lachlan said.

From the top of the glen there appeared what Innis had been half expecting.

Wolves.

He counted eight of them. The animals entered the valley at a run and then slowed and seemed to relax, as if they were home now. Every wolf had black fur and the biggest one was the animal that Innis had encountered three time before. His wolf.

This one was definitely the alpha male, the leader of the pack. He stayed alert, standing above the pack on the slope of the hill while the other wolves slouched down or began to play. Three of the wolves were smaller and they chased each other; the rest licked their fur or snuffled the ground or just lay and yawned, showing their sharp teeth.

'That's a lot of wolves,' Innis said, astonished.

'Only half of them,' said Lachlan. 'They're moving in two different packs now. The other pack will have already gone to ground.'

Innis watched the wolves for five minutes and then the big wolf began to lope down the glen. The others rose as one and followed. They entered the birch wood at the valley bottom, the big wolf lingering at the edge of the trees. It turned and seemed to Innis to look straight at him. The wolf raised its head and emitted a single howl. It darted into the small forest and was gone.

'No way,' said Lachlan.

'What?'

'They never howl. It's safer for them not to.' Lachlan stared at Innis with a look of confused wonder. 'That howl was for you.'

'Where've they gone?'

'They're resting. They've been feeding and socializing but now it's time for sleep. There's an ancient badger sett in the trees that they've taken over and enlarged. It gives them triple protection; concealed underground, among the trees, in a secret glen. No one would ever know they're there.'

Innis couldn't get his head around how there could be a pack of wolves hiding in a secret glen. 'When did you release them? How did they find this place?'

'I've never said the wolves were released. That was you.'

'So . . . where have they come from?'

Lachlan offered a rare smile. 'They haven't come from anywhere. They've always been here.'

The boy reached into his pocket and pulled out a sheet of folded paper. He smoothed it out and handed it to Innis.

'An old map?' Innis said.

'Just a colour copy, but aye, it's an old map. It's a section of Herman Moll's map of the Western Isles. Published in 1745.'

'That's the year of the Jacobite rising. When Bonnie Prince Charlie came to Scotland.'

'Aye, and it's likely this was the map that guided him around.'

Innis looked carefully. 'It's a map of Nin.'

'What do you see?'

Innis scanned the map. The island town was there – marked *Sculavag* – and there were a few other named features, including the big mountain.

'There's *Beinn Ainmhidhean*.'

'The Hill of the Beasts, aye. And what else do you see?'

Innis peered at the map. Just beside the mountain there was other writing; tiny and swirling and hard to read. It marked the steep hill above the hidden glen.

'How's your Gaelic?' Lachlan asked.

'Not great. But I know this word.' Innis was beginning to grasp what Lachlan was showing him. He felt that familiar tingle run up his spine. 'The hill where we're sitting had a name.'

Lachlan turned towards him, a look of shared under-standing on his face. 'Aye.'

'It was called *Cnoc Madaidhean-allaidh*. The Rise of Wolves.'

Lachlan nodded. 'It has always been the hill of the wolf.'

'That's new to me. Did it lose its name when the wolves died out?'

Lachlan took back the map and replaced it in his pocket. 'You still don't get it, do you?'

'Get what?' Innis asked.

'It's said that the last wild wolf was killed in Scotland in 1743, at the river Findhorn in Moray.'

'Two years before the Bonnie Prince landed in Scotland.'

'Aye, but we know that's not true. In fact, someone claimed to have seen a wild wolf in Sutherland as late as 1888.'

'Doubtful,' Innis said.

'Maybe not.'

Innis knew now what Lachlan was telling him. It seemed far too incredible to be true. 'You're not saying . . .' He couldn't find the words. 'You can't be serious . . .'

Lachlan nodded gravely. 'Wolves died out on the mainland, aye, but the wild wolf never went completely extinct. On remote islands it clung on for a while, until eventually only one population remained.'

Innis said quietly, 'The wolves of Nin.'

'The wolves here in the glen, the wolves you've seen on the island. Those are the last wild wolves in Scotland.'

Chapter 29

Innis had lost the power of speech. He seemed to have forgotten how to breathe as well.

'I know it sounds like nonsense,' Lachlan said, 'but you have to believe me. The wolves aren't from the wildlife sanctuary, we haven't released them to roam the Barrens. They've been running wild, those ones and their ancestors, since the end of the last ice age.'

Innis forced out some words. 'Someone must have spotted them.'

'People did, people still do occasionally, but they think they're dogs or that they imagined it or they describe what they saw and nobody believes them.'

'Been there.' Innis remembered Kat's sceptical face. 'But how have they survived?'

'Wolves are very secretive anyway, but this lot have

adapted their lifestyle to remain hidden. Their coats turned black. They don't howl. They hunt at night, live underground and use caves as breeding dens. They very rarely leave their glen or the small hills surrounding it. They certainly wouldn't venture on to the Barrens during the day.' Lachlan paused and his eyebrows dipped in a frown. 'Until now.'

'I walked across the Barrens so many times. I never once saw a wolf.'

'They've started coming on to the moor. It's got something to do with your leap. I think they know somehow that you're the next Laird of Nin.'

Innis snorted. 'I haven't even leapt yet.'

Lachlan gave a grim laugh. 'I think the wolves are telling you to get on with it.'

Innis sat for a moment, looking down into the valley, trying to digest this massive revelation. 'Is that what your uncle meant when he said I'm the one?'

'There has always been a belief in our family, passed down through generations, that the wolves would tell us who was to be the next Laird of Nin.' For a moment, Lachlan looked desperately sad. 'We even hoped it might be me.'

'It could still be you. You can do the leap.'

The boy sighed and smiled. 'No, the wolves have spoken. Or rather, they've howled.'

'How do you know all this? How do *you* know about the wolves when no one else does?'

'It's the family business. We've been entrusted with looking after the wolves of Nin for almost three hundred years. It was a job given to us by Bonnie Prince Charlie himself.'

'No!'

'Yep. When the wolves of Nin helped the Prince escape he made the then Laird of Nin promise to protect the creatures. There were barely any wolves left in Scotland already. And of course, these were special animals. They could recognize a King.'

'But that's just a legend.'

'Every legend has truth in it somewhere. The Laird employed my ancestor, Hamish Geddes, to look after the wolves. My family have safeguarded them ever since, even after the last Laird of Nin died. There was money put aside to allow the work to continue.' Lachlan gave a laugh. 'You and Kat were not the first Guardians of Nin.'

'So the whole wildlife sanctuary thing is just a ruse?' Innis asked.

'No, we're doing useful work there, breeding wildcats and the like, but our main job is protecting the wolves.'

'But why keep them secret? Surely they would be safer if people knew about them?'

'If people knew about the wolves Nin would become one big safari park. Or more likely, the wolves would be taken off the island and put in zoos "for their own protection". And then the wild wolf, the properly *wild* wolf, would truly have gone extinct. We can't take that risk; the animals have to stay on Nin and stay hidden. That was the agreement that the Laird made with my family. The belief was that when the wolves disappeared the Lairds of Nin would follow.'

'But there's not been a Laird of Nin for hundreds of years.'

'We've been waiting for the right man.'

'How is this connected with the leap?'

'We tried to keep that quiet as well. Otherwise every idiot would be giving it a go and falling to his death. No, first the wolves would pick their champion and then that man would prove himself worthy by leaping the gap.'

'The Lord of the Leap. So why me? I just tripped over the stone.'

'It had begun long before that. You were the Boy of the Barrens. That's the name my uncle gave you. And remember, before you ever discovered the stone you heard the howling of the wolves.'

'If I'm the Boy of the Barrens, who are you?'

'I'm the next in line of wolf protectors. My uncle is the oldest brother, but he has no family of his own. Someone was needed to take over the job when he was gone. I came to Nin at the start of the year to learn the family business. Unfortunately I'm still not old enough to leave school ...'

'You're hardly there anyway.'

'That's because I'm needed here on Nin, watching out for the wolves. Especially now with all this wind turbine stuff going on.'

'The school doesn't know any of this?'

'No. They think I moved to Skye to stay with my sister. They know nothing about Nin.'

'That explains the wee caravan.'

'I couldn't stay in the stupid hostel. There'd be too many question when I wasn't there.'

Innis exhaled a long dumbfounded breath and tried to make sense of all that he had been told.

'Why tell me now? About the wolves I mean.'

'We could hardly deny it. Not to you. And we need you to do your leap.'

'But you've been so against the idea. You tried to throw me off the ferry.'

'It's not the leap that's the problem. It's the circus that's coming with it. You were just supposed to leap, no fuss involved. Instead, you're bringing the world to watch.'

'Sorry,' Innis said quietly.

'And all this wind turbine activity isn't helping. The wolves and the workers are bound to come together.'

Innis looked at Lachlan. *As long as he's telling truths, then he might tell all of it*, he thought. 'Is that why you sabotaged their equipment?'

'I told you, that wasn't me. I've been busy following the wolves.'

'That's why you were off school last week?'

Lachlan gave a weary nod. 'I've been trying to prevent any contact between man and animal. Though they kept finding *you*. The turbine people have mostly gone now. A decision has been reached – we've just found out that we lost our last appeal against eviction. In two weeks' time the wildlife sanctuary gets flattened. If that happens and the wolves are discovered, then that's the end of them. That's why you have to do your leap. You have to be Laird of Nin. That's the only way to save the Barrens. If we can save the Barrens, the wolves stay hidden.'

If doing the leap had been important before, it had taken on a whole new level of significance. There was so much more at stake now than just his grandfather's health and Kat's dark skies. Now Innis had wolves to protect. And yet, by trying to save the animals he risked dooming them. The leap had become a must-see event. There were a bunch of people coming to the empty portion of the island where the animals roamed. All of which meant loads of opportunities for someone carrying a smartphone to come across a wolf and change everything, for ever.

Because of him there was a very real possibility that the last wild wolves in Scotland were about to be discovered.

Chapter 30

Thursday morning was cloaked in a grey sky as Innis and Kat walked through the wildlife sanctuary. The place seemed to be crumbling already, and Innis wondered what would happen to the other animals once the bulldozers arrived. He hadn't wanted to ask Lachlan; the wolves seemed enough of a worry. Kat and Innis had left him feeding the wildcats.

'This way,' Innis said, and Kat followed him down the slight hill towards the ocean.

'I can't believe Lachlan didn't kill you,' she said.

'I did what you asked. I fixed it.'

'How?'

'Never mind.' Lachlan and he had a shared secret now. That was the difference.

'But you seem, I dunno, almost *friends*.'

Innis gave her a smile. 'I wouldn't go that far.'

As Kat smiled in return he still couldn't shake the feeling that it was her who had struck the match two days earlier, setting fire to the truck. Today she had asked to see the leap and he wondered if she was trying to work out which plan to save the Barrens had the best chance of success. He had to convince her burning everything in sight was not the way to go, but he couldn't even bring himself to ask if she was the saboteur.

They stepped out on to the cliff and walked along the path until the edge dropped away, leaving a large gap to the other side. From the space between came the boom of the waves channelled between the breach in the rock face. Kat moved cautiously to the edge and peered over, then moved quickly back. She stared mournfully at the cleft.

'Is this it?' she asked.

'The Bonnie Laddie's Leap.'

'It's too far.'

'It looks further than it is.'

'No, it's every bit as far as it looks.' She glared at Innis with panicked eyes. 'You'll never jump that gap.'

'I'm not going to jump.' Innis gave a flourishing wave of the arms. 'I am going to *leap*.'

'This isn't funny. This really isn't funny. That gap is far too big to jump across.'

'It's not, I measured it.'

'Then we'll have to measure it again. Wait here.'

Kat strode away from the cliff edge. Innis looked

again – the gap did seem rather wide. A trick of the light, he told himself. He could do this. He *had* to do it. There was even more depending on it now.

Kat was back, with Lachlan in tow. She held up a tape measure.

'Let's see, shall we?'

'But I measured it already,' Innis said. 'One hundred and ninety centimetres. Just short of two metres.'

The girl positioned Lachlan at one side of the cleft and handed him the tape measure. 'Stand here and hold this tight.'

Kat began pulling the metal strip from its housing. She walked the length of the gap, unspooling until she reached the other side. She pinched the tape between her fingers and stared at the measurement. The metal tape swung slightly in the wind as it stretched between Lachlan and the girl. Innis looked the length of it and it seemed longer than he remembered. He heard Kat say,

'Oh God.'

She walked back towards him slowly, the tape sliding back into its housing. She had a face of dread.

'One hundred and ninety centimetres?' Innis asked hopefully.

Kat shook her head.

He wasn't good with numbers, he should have realized that. 'How far off was I?'

'The number is fine,' she said.

'So what's the problem?'

'It's your unit of measurement.'

'I don't understand.'

'The gap doesn't measure one hundred and ninety centimetres. It measures one hundred and ninety *inches*. You read the wrong markings.'

'And what difference does that make?'

Kat gave a deep and desperate sigh. 'Oh Innis, it makes a world of difference.'

There was silence for a moment. Innis could hear the crash of waves against the cliff beneath him. The boom seemed louder now. Louder and closer.

'How big a difference?' he asked quietly.

Kat looked him coldly in the eye. 'One hundred and ninety inches is almost five metres. Two and half times the distance you thought it was.'

Innis's reply was hesitant. 'I think I could jump that.'

Kat clenched her fists in despair. 'If you were a half-decent long jumper you could probably get enough distance. If you were a reasonable sprinter you could maybe get enough speed. If you were a passable high jumper you could possibly get enough height. You are none of these things. Not even close. And no amount of practice is going to teach you to fly.'

Innis leant forwards and looked over the edge of what now seemed an impossible leap. Up to this point his dyscalculia had been a pain, an inconvenience, a minor problem to be ignored or occasionally overcome. Now his number blindness had led to a mistake so calamitous it would bring about the end of him. He had announced his intention to leap and told the world the distance wasn't far.

Turned out that it was.

'It will be a bit embarrassing for you at first,' Kat said, 'but people will understand.'

'I'll look a fool. Even more of a fool than I do already.'

'Better a live fool than a dead one.'

'Thanks for that.'

'You have to try,' Lachlan said, giving a look that asked Innis to remember the secret they shared. 'I think you can make it.'

Kat spat her words. 'You can't just *give it a go*! There's no trial run, no changing your mind halfway across. There's a reason those three other men died. The distance is too far.'

'What about your dark skies?' Lachlan asked. 'This might be your last hope.'

'I'm not giving up on them just yet. This, though –' she jabbed a finger towards the chasm – 'this would be madness.'

Kat moved away. Lachlan sighed and followed her. Innis was left alone on the cliff edge with only a crushing sense of failure for company. He had let everyone down. For a moment, he considered just going for it, right here, right now, run and leap and see what happened. He peered over the edge and watched the waves break against the rocks far below and knew exactly what would happen.

He turned and trudged away from the cliff, back towards his old life of insignificance. No longer Lord of the Leap. Now just Lord of the Quit.

Back home that afternoon, Innis plonked himself on to his bed and picked up his tablet. He'd made a point of avoiding it before, but now he clicked on to affyerheid.com. The Graveheart tour seemed to be in full swing. The first stunt had involved a man swimming naked across Loch Ness with a mass of rotting fish stuck to his body. The comments were full of disappointment that he hadn't been eaten by the monster, ignoring the fact that he had nearly died of hypothermia. The guy who had tried to scale the Old Man of Storr without a rope hadn't got very far before falling and breaking bones. Just as well, as climbing any higher might have resulted in even more dire consequences. As it was, the website stated that doctors were confident he would walk again.

Innis clicked the close button. People swimming naked in search of Nessie, people climbing up high rocks without a rope, people leaping over wide chasms to own an island. Lachlan had called it a circus and the clowns always got the biggest cheer. He was well out of it.

How to tell Matt McGowan.

He opened his email, found the correct recipient and started typing.

Sorry Matt, I can't do the Bonnie Laddie's Leap.

Short and to the point. Innis hit send. He sat for a

moment contemplating the screen and almost instantly a message fired back. It was from Matt.

What's the problem?

Innis pondered for a moment. Lachlan had said the wolves had chosen him for the leap, but clearly the wolves couldn't measure either. He had to be honest.

I'm not going to make it, it's too far.

There, he had admitted it, sent it into cyberspace to be hacked and trolled and unfollowed. Matt replied.

Come on, that's not the attitude. Think positive.

Easy for him to say; Matt's only concern was getting a sufficient number of likes.

I measured it wrong. The gap is further than I thought. It can't be done.

I think you should still give it a go.

What had Matt McGowan not understood?

I will die.

There, black and white, no doubt about it, unequivocal.

You probably won't die. Sure, there's a bit of a risk – but that's what makes it exciting.

He 'probably' wouldn't die! Innis sat back in his chair and stared at the words on the screen. Now he saw the harsh truth. Whether he succeeded or failed was not a concern for Matt McGowan. Both made good viewing.

He had to be blunt.

I won't do it.

Innis waited for a response.

You kind of have to.

Why?

You signed a contract.

I'm just a schoolboy. No one will hold me to it.

Your mother countersigned it.

Innis leant forward in the chair and put his head in his hands. At the time he didn't think it would matter if he forged his mother's signature. Where was the harm?

I forged her signature.

That's what you say. I have a signed document. You should have read the small print.

Innis sighed. Always read the small print.

What was in it?

It states quite clearly that if you pull out you will have to reimburse any monies already paid, both fees to yourself and money spent on preparations.

This was not looking good. Maybe it wouldn't be too much money in the end.

How much money would I have to – Innis looked at Matt's message for the word – *reimburse if I pulled out?*

There was a minute's pause, and he wondered if Matt McGowan was making calculations or just making him sweat.

There is the £500 you asked me to donate to your wind turbine campaign as a fee. Add to that about another £2000 in publicity and admin and billed hours. I can give you a detailed invoice later if you like but it will be around £2500.

Innis didn't reply. He sat rigid in his chair, his eyes no longer focused on the screen, his mind no longer focused on anything, just a swirl of thoughts about where he could possibly get that kind of money. Another message popped up.

Do you have that kind of money?

No.

Best just do the leap, eh?

What choice did he have? He didn't have the money. Would they repossess his croft if he didn't pay up, turf him and Gramps out on to the street? It wasn't even a street, just a dirt track. With heavy fingers, Innis typed.

Okay.

Chapter 31

Someone knocked hard on the door of the croft, and Innis peeled himself from the armchair by the fire. He plodded to the door and wearily pulled it open. Kat stood there.

'Are you ready to go?' she asked.

'Go where?'

'The meeting.'

'What meeting?'

Kat threw her hands up in the air. 'The town meeting with the wind turbine people.'

'I'd forgotten about that.'

There were other troubles occupying his thoughts. Matt McGowan had pressured him into doing the leap regardless of distance or chance of success. He had spent the afternoon trying to devise a plan that might get him out of it. Nothing cunning had come to mind.

'I don't think I'll bother,' he said.

'Of course you're coming.'

'It will just be a bunch of people talking.'

'Exactly, that's why we have to go. We need to put across our point of view.' Innis's face scrunched at the thought. 'Now that Plan B is a definite bust, this is all we've got,' Kat added.

This was not the moment to tell her that Plan B was still on. Gramps appeared from his bedroom wearing shoes and jacket.

'Let's go lad,' he said, giving Kat a wink.

They piled into the Land Rover and headed for town. When they parked at the harbour there was already a stream of people heading up the hill towards the Fishermen's Mission. Innis let his grandfather lean on his arm as they moved in the same direction.

The hall was set out with rows of chairs and at the far wall was a table with a microphone and projector. Kat's mum found a seat for his grandfather at the back. Innis stood by the wall and tried to blend into the cracked plasterwork. He had already spotted a few eyes looking at him and some pointing and whispers. Kat was seated in the front row. Near the middle sat Dougal Geddes. There was no sign of Lachlan.

The meeting started and a spokesman from the local council talked about clean energy and job creation and the economic boost that would come to the island.

Everyone in the room quietly watched. No one was disputing that wind energy was a good thing.

It was only when a woman from the company stood up and gave a slide show revealing how the Barrens would be transformed that an occasional murmur could be heard. She emphasized how the environment would be protected and showed a picture of how the moor would look after completion. It was very pleasant and futuristic, with trees planted and nature walks and windmills stretching into the distance. But it wasn't the Barrens.

Innis thought, *The wolves have no chance.*

After the presentation, the man from the council offered the audience the opportunity to ask questions. Innis watched Kat hesitantly raise a hand. Hers was the only one, so the council man pointed in her direction.

'Can I just ask this question?' Kat's voice was nervous and hard to hear.

The energy woman sighed and gave a curt 'Yes', as if young girls shouldn't be asking questions.

Innis saw Kat swallow hard.

'Do you care at all what the people of Nin think?'

The woman looked insulted. 'Of course we do. That is why we're having this meeting, to answer your questions and listen to your views.'

'Then if the view of most islanders is that the Barrens is not the place for your turbines, why not put them somewhere else? Why not offshore, out of the way?'

'There are maintenance issues and cost implications

with siting them offshore.'

'So your decision is based simply on money.'

'That's not what I said.'

Kat was warming up. 'But profit is more important than the opinion of the islanders?'

The woman seemed slightly flustered. 'Again, you may be putting words in my mouth.'

'So the opinion of the islanders *is* more important than profit? Is that what you are saying?'

The woman's dilemma was how to counter an angry thirteen-year-old girl without seeming like a bully. 'There are many considerations to be made.'

'But nobody wants turbines on the Barrens. What else do you need to know?'

The woman seemed unsure how to respond. Kat seemed to have the victory, but then the harbour master interjected. Mr Wallace stood up from his seat close to the front.

'Actually lass, there are some on Nin who feel the island's remote interior is the most suitable location for the turbines.'

Kat threw the harbour master a glance of fury.

The company woman smiled. 'As you see, opinions are divided.'

'But what about the dark skies?' said Kat. 'They'll be ruined.'

'You can still have your dark skies. The wind turbines don't emit light in themselves.'

'But each one will have a flashing red light at the top.'

'That's necessary, as a warning for aircraft.'

'And the base of each turbine will be lit?'

'A soft light, for emergency access.'

Kat had done her homework. 'And access roads will have lighting?'

'A little, not too much.'

'It will be enough. Enough to ruin it.'

'You will still be able to see your stars,' the woman said.

'But we won't be a dark sky community. It won't be the same. It won't be as good.' Innis thought he heard a bubble in her throat. 'It won't be perfect.'

'We appreciate your concerns, but a little light pollution is not sufficient reason to rule out the central and northern portion of the island as the site for our development.'

Innis looked at his grandfather. There was a deep frown across his face and his hands were trembling as they sat on his lap.

'So a final decision has been reached?' Kat asked.

'Yes, it has,' said the man from the council.

'But what about our protests?'

The woman gave a smug smile. 'A few posters and some T-shirts does not a movement make.'

Innis saw his grandfather struggle to his feet. He moved across to help, wondering where Gramps was going. The woman continued.

'And all this nonsense, letting air out of tyres and

dismantling equipment, it won't change our decision.'

In a clear voice, Gramps said, 'It is a small sign of the passion some feel about protecting and conserving the beauty of the Barrens.'

'Well, one man's passion is another man's vandalism.'

No one spoke for a moment, there was whispering around the room. If Kat had hoped to influence the outcome, it hadn't happened.

Innis's grandfather cleared his throat. 'Tell me this, lass,' he said, 'who is it that owns the land on which you wish to build your monstrosities?'

The two spokespeople at the front glanced at each other, and the man from the council said, 'No one owns the land as such. The land is held in trust, and we, as a council, have the right to administer it as we see best. That includes leasing the area and giving planning permission for development. Which we have done in this case.'

Innis didn't like where this was heading.

Gramps asked, 'And why is there no landowner?'

The council man hesitated. Did he also suspect where the conversation was going?

'The former owner of the land, the twelfth Laird of Nin, died without issue and no heir was found. He made some specifications about who should succeed to the title and property but these were never fulfilled and the land remains in trust.'

'But if these requirements were to be fulfilled?'

Innis *really* didn't like where this conversation was heading.

The man rubbed his chin and looked to the woman from the company, who returned his look with a wide-eyed stare. He cast his eyes down, examining nothing in particular on the table in front of him.

'I am not completely versed in the legal particulars. I wouldn't like to speculate on matters of this nature.'

Innis looked to his grandfather, hoping he would sit down now. He saw the man's face and knew that wasn't going to happen. With a trembling hand, Gramps grabbed Innis's arm.

'This lad is Innis Munro. He is my grandson. And on Saturday coming he is going to make the Bonnie Laddie's Leap.' Gramps looked carefully at the two people sitting silently at the front. 'And by doing so, as I'm sure you are both aware, he will become the thirteenth Laird of Nin. And as such he will be the owner of the land referred to as the Barrens.'

Innis felt his stomach contents begin to make their way towards his throat. Gramps turned and smacked him on the back.

'Isn't that right, lad?'

The murmur in the room became an excited babble. Innis forced a weak smile. A few voices rose from the hub-bub. 'Nice one, Innis.' 'Go on yourself, lad.' 'You can do it, son.'

Innis eyed the people at the front. The council man

looked despondent and the company woman looked furious. Innis glanced at Kat. She sat with her head in her hands. He looked back at his grandfather.

'We're depending on you, lad,' he said. 'It's up to you to save the Barrens.'

Chapter 32

Gramps was in bed and Innis was staring at the fire when his phone beeped. It was a message from Kat. *Come and see this.* He stepped quietly from the croft out into the dark. There was a chill to the air and as he looked up at the clear night sky he knew why Kat had summoned him. The aurora borealis, the Northern Lights. The sky was glistening green.

Innis walked to the girl's garden. Her telescope was out but she was sitting on the wall, head back, enraptured by the sight.

'Isn't it wonderful?' she said as he approached.

'Aye, it looks amazing tonight.'

The sky glowed with green light that moved in waves across the horizon. Pulses of purple ignited the ether at its edges. Shimmers of yellow radiated across the heavens like a solar flare. And then it returned to radiate green, as if the sky was lit by the beams of a billion lightsabers.

'Isn't it incredible?' Kat said, finding a different word. 'I first saw the Northern Lights when I was seven and it was the most magical thing I had ever seen.'

Innis had heard this story a hundred times, but he liked to hear her tell it.

'I had to know why it was happening, why the dark sky was lit like a rainbow. My dad could only say it was something to do with the solar wind. So that same night I refused to go to bed until I knew. We searched on the internet, and you remember how bad the broadband connection was back then. We were buffering until midnight.'

'It *is* very pretty.'

'It's not just pretty, it is a scientific wonder.' Innis nodded in silence before Kat added, 'So then, explain it to me.'

She was teasing him and testing him.

'Something to do with the solar wind.'

She smiled sadly, the mood too sombre to muster a laugh. 'Charged particles from the sun strike atoms in the atmosphere. Electrons in the atoms move from low energy to high energy and then back again. This releases photons, and these photons produce light. Wonderful coloured light of every tone and hue.'

'Isn't that what I said?'

They sat in silence for a while and enjoyed the light

show. At last the display faded and the sky returned to black.

'That was amazing,' Kat said, lowering herself from the wall and moving to her telescope. 'I'm looking at the moon up close, if you want to see.'

'I can see it fine from here, thanks.'

'Suit yourself.' She looked for a moment then said, 'I'm going to go there someday. I'll bring you back a piece of moon rock.'

'Whoopie doo,' he said.

Kat smiled. 'What would *you* do with a piece of moon rock?'

'I would sell it on eBay and buy something useful, something that's not just a piece of rock.'

Kat gave an unconvincing frown. 'One day, I'll also go to Mars.'

'I'm going to have an impressive rock collection.'

'You joke, but it'll be someone our age today who, in twenty or thirty years, will be first to descend from the Mars lander on to the planet's surface. And that person will not be a test pilot this time, that person will be a scientist or engineer. And that person will be a woman.'

'You think?'

'I know. If you found me a rocket I would go right now.'

Innis laughed. 'If I found a rocket I would keep it for myself. A rocket would be useful. Get me the height I need for the leap.'

Kat gave him a sympathetic smile. 'Your grandfather will understand. The distance is too far. Throwing yourself to your death won't help anyone.'

Innis sighed. 'My grandfather has put the fate of the Barrens completely on to me. How do I not let him down?'

'By not dying.'

'There is also the slight problem of two thousand five hundred pounds that I owe the website people.'

There was silence, and Innis waited and hoped that Kat might have a good idea. In the end, all she said was, 'What are you going to do?'

Innis shrugged. 'The easiest solution would be just to go for it. See what happens. With a strong wind at my back and legs full of adrenalin, I might just make it.'

Kat lifted herself from the telescope and looked at him with her most serious face. 'A hurricane at your back wouldn't blow you over that gap. It can't be done.'

Innis could only shake his head.

He was in a bind all right. Matt McGowan was telling him he *had* to do the leap. Lachlan was telling him he *had* to do the leap. Now Gramps was telling him he *had* to do the leap. Kat was telling him he couldn't possibly do the leap, even though it might be the only hope to save her dark skies. What was his heart telling him? *Just go for it, be Lord of the Leap.* What was his head telling him? *Don't be daft.*

Kat was peering through her telescope again.

'There's a hundred billion stars in the Milky Way,' she

said. 'Our sun is just one of them. How many earth-like planets must there be in our galaxy alone? Who is out there right now, watching us watching them?'

Innis's eyes peered first at the sky and then out towards the Barrens.

'Probably some goon from the energy company, waiting for us to set fire to another truck.'

He looked at Kat, hoping for a guilty reaction, but she gave nothing away. He wanted to ask her if she was the fire-raising saboteur but something held him back; the fear that if he was wrong she would never forgive him for thinking such a thing.

Kat moved from the telescope. 'Someone came and took the burnt one away.'

'Did they say anything about who did it?'

'Not a word. They don't care any more. The decision has been made.' There was defeat in her voice. 'The Barrens will be the site for the wind turbines.' Her shoulders sagged. 'Oh Innis, what can we do?'

Innis sighed and shook his head. The leap would save everything, but without it he could do nothing to prevent the wind turbines, nothing to help Gramps be comfortable in his final days, nothing to save Kat's dark skies and bright stars. And without the leap the wolves were doomed.

'We continue with the protest,' he said, 'we get a petition started. There's lots we can do.'

Kat slowly shook her head. 'No, posters and petitions

won't work. We need something else. Something they can't ignore. If we want to protect the dark skies of Nin we need something much more dramatic.' It was as if an idea was coming to her as she spoke.

Oh God, thought Innis. There was something in that look; a narrowing of the eyes, a set of the chin, a purse of the lips. She had a new plan, a *backed into a corner and this is the only way out* kind of plan. She wanted something more dramatic, as if a burning pickup wasn't dramatic enough.

'You've got to stop this,' he said. 'That's not the way. Whatever you are planning, don't do it. You could end up in prison.'

Kat gave him the strangest of stares, as if he had gone mad. 'What are you talking about?'

'I know it's you who has been doing the sabotage, not Lachlan. I don't know what you have in mind, what you would consider *more dramatic*, but someone might get hurt next time – it's just not worth it.'

The girl snorted, then snarled. 'Seriously?'

'Well if it wasn't Lachlan . . .'

Kat gave the longest sigh. 'Thanks, Innis.'

'What's your plan then?'

'It doesn't involve setting fire to anything. It's much simpler than that.' She laughed, as if astonished that no one had thought of it before. 'The Barrens will protect themselves.'

'What do you mean?'

'I wouldn't do it if there was any other way.'

She lifted her telescope and folded up the tripod legs.

'What's your plan?' Innis asked again.

'I'll talk to you in the morning.' The girl headed back to her croft, carrying the telescope. She disappeared inside and the back door clicked shut.

Innis stood in the garden, the dark sky glittering above his head. It wasn't the twinkling of stars that worried him. It was the twinkle in her eye. *That* twinkle. What did she mean, *the Barrens will protect themselves*? What was her plan now?

Whatever it was, he was certain he wasn't going to like it.

Chapter 33

Innis awoke to the sound of rain drumming on the roof of his croft. He hunkered under his duvet. This was a morning for staying in bed, although he knew he would have to face the day at some point. If the leap was off then an announcement had to be made. All those people coming to the island to see the show had to be stopped, and he had to work out how to raise £2500. If the leap was still on, as expected by Matt and by Gramps, then he had to work out how to jump an impossible gap. It hurt his head to think about it. The duvet was the best option.

He must have fallen asleep again because the next thing he knew he was wakened by another tapping sound. Not the rain this time.

Someone was knocking at the front door.

Innis jumped out of bed, glancing at his digital clock. It said 7.42. As he made his way through the living room he saw his grandfather emerge sleepily from his bedroom.

'I've got this, Gramps,' he said.

The knock came again and Innis took a peek out the window to see who it was. Lachlan Geddes was standing in the rain. Innis quickly opened the door. Lachlan had never come calling before.

'We need to talk,' Lachlan said.

Innis watched big beads of rain drip from Lachlan's bedraggled face. The wind was swirling in the doorway and getting Innis wet as well. Gramps said, 'Bring the laddie in.'

Innis stepped back and let Lachlan enter the croft.

'Take off your jacket,' Gramps said. 'Warm yourself by the fire. I'll make us a cup of tea.'

Lachlan did as he was asked and sat on a chair by the flame that Gramps had coaxed to life. He rubbed his hands together in the warmth.

As Gramps filled the kettle he said, 'And what's your name, lad?'

'I'm Lachlan. We've met before, when we were up the . . .' Innis shook his head and Lachlan said nothing more.

'Lachlan is a friend from school, Gramps.' It sounded strange to say it. Innis had never had friends round before.

'Is that right?' the old man said. 'And you're a Nin boy?'

'Not originally, but I am now.'

'Grand, that's grand.'

As the kettle boiled Gramps disappeared into his bedroom.

'I don't think he remembers you,' Innis said.

'Sorry, I didn't realize.'

'His memory comes and goes, like his tremors. It's not going to get better.'

'I'm sorry.'

For a moment, the only sounds were the boiling kettle, the crackle of peat in the hearth and the rain blowing hard against the croft.

'So, have you talked to Kat?' Innis asked.

'Kat? No, why do you ask that?'

'She said she had another plan to save the Barrens. Wouldn't tell me what it was.'

'I've heard nothing.'

Innis stared into the fire. He had already falsely accused Lachlan of being the saboteur. He didn't want to accuse another innocent person. But it had to be said.

'Do you think it could be Kat who's doing the vandalism?'

Lachlan looked surprised. 'I don't know. I wouldn't think so. Do you?'

'I'm not sure. Maybe.' He looked at Lachlan and shrugged. 'I'm worried it might be Kat and she's planning something else, something even more dramatic than setting fire to a truck.'

'That wouldn't be good.'

'No.'

'But it's okay,' Lachlan said, 'It won't be necessary. We'll just stick to the earlier plan. The earlier plan will work.'

'What earlier plan?'

Lachlan offered a sly smile. 'You have to do your leap.'

Innis snorted. 'We already know that's the worst idea.'

'But the leap is the perfect plan. If you make it you become Laird of Nin. Then the Barrens belong to you and the wind turbines go elsewhere. Kat's stars will still be there, the wolves will stay undiscovered, you get a castle. Everybody wins.'

'I don't really want a castle. Anyway, there is the one big problem.'

Lachlan nodded. 'I know. You'll never make it across the gap. But what if I told you there is a way to do your leap and make it to the other side. Alive.'

'How?'

'It's why I came here this morning.'

'Tell me.'

'Better if I show you.'

Twenty minutes later, Innis was clinging to the back of the quad bike as Lachlan bounced it up the track towards the wildlife sanctuary. The rain still flung itself to the ground and Innis was soaked, despite his waterproof jacket. When they arrived, they clambered off the quad and Innis pulled at his wet trousers while Lachlan pushed the bike into a building and out of the rain. When he re-emerged he said simply, 'This way.'

Innis followed, and as they walked past the wildcat enclosure Lachlan stopped.

'It's not a complete ruse,' he said. 'The work we're doing with wildcats is of national importance. But even that will end if they demolish this place.'

'Couldn't the whole of Nin become a wildlife sanctuary? The wolves would be safe then.'

'In an ideal world, aye, but there would always be someone wanting a selfie with a wild Scottish wolf. Or some idiot wanting to bag one for his trophy cabinet. Nin is a small place, it'd end up a zoo and nothing more. If the wolves can't roam free, if they're constantly disturbed and examined, then they'll no longer be wild. And my family will have failed.'

'Well, you better tell me *your* plan then.'

Lachlan said nothing, but led Innis along the cliff edge until they got to the spot of the Bonnie Laddie's Leap. The boy stood contemplating the rolling ocean that Innis could hear but not see from where he stood. Lachlan stared across the wide gap to the other side.

'You honestly thought you could leap this?'

Innis edged closer, peered anew at the chasm that was the Bonnie Laddie's Leap. It looked further than it had ever looked before and he felt his stomach churn at his stupidity.

'You said the wolves had chosen me. Why choose me if I was never going to make it?'

Lachlan laughed. 'The problem is, a wolf could leap that gap. You're just a boy with skinny legs.'

'So how do my skinny legs get across then?'

'Who's been out here?' Lachlan asked.

'Where?'

'Right here at the leap.'

'Just me and Kat. And you. No one else.'

'Good.' Lachlan smiled. 'Good.'

'What are you thinking?'

'I looked at the photos you posted. Nice ones of the stone, but there's not much of the leap itself. You see a bit of the water, a bit of the cliff.'

'I didn't want to get too close to the edge. I don't like heights.'

'Says the Lord of the Leap.' Lachlan smiled again. 'It's good. It's exactly what we need.'

'For what?'

'I'll show you.'

Lachlan began walking along the cliff edge and Innis followed. A hundred metres further on he stopped, sweeping a hand across the drop towards the sea.

'Here it is. The Bonnie Laddie's Leap – mark two.'

There was another cleft in the rock, much narrower than the Leap. There were no sharp rocks at the base, just a channel of deep, dark water.

Lachlan said, 'We move the stone, we call *this* the

Bonnie Laddie's Leap. It looks similar, it's in the right location. It is just a whole lot narrower.'

'How much narrower?'

'It is one hundred and eighty-two centimetres. Just under two metres.'

'I've jumped that distance in training.'

'Exactly. This one can be done.'

'But my training jump wasn't across a deep drop with the ocean below.'

'Aye, there's still an element of risk to it. But it wouldn't be convincing if there wasn't still the chance you could die. It'll keep your website guy happy.'

It was genius – Innis couldn't believe he hadn't thought of this before. He laughed at the audacity of it. 'That's brilliant. It seems so obvious now.'

'It's cheating a bit, but at this point, do we care? Big picture and all that.'

'You're right. The end result is the important thing. Does it really matter how we get there?'

Innis's heart was thumping hard in his chest. He could do this, he could leap the Bonnie Laddie's Leap and become Laird of Nin. But then he had a thought, a dampener.

'People will still come to watch. They'll cross the Barrens to get here. The wolves might be discovered anyway.'

'I've thought of a way to deal with that. You just concentrate on getting across that gap. You can do this.'

'Aye, I think I can.'

Innis's phone beeped and he pulled it from his pocket, swiped it open and read the text message.

'I knew she was up to something,' he said.

'What is it?' asked Lachlan.

'It's a message from Matt McGowan. He's on the island. He's asking how I know a girl called Katrina McColl. Apparently, she's on her way to meet him in town, says she has something very interesting to tell him. Something that will make everything else on his website just clickbait.' Innis sighed. 'What's she setting fire to now?'

He looked at Lachlan, and Lachlan looked aghast.

'That's not it,' the boy groaned.

'What?'

Lachlan rubbed his forehead, took a moment to speak.

'Yesterday, after we measured the leap and Kat came down hard on you, I thought she needed to know why it was so important that you give it a go. I thought she needed to know the truth.'

'What did you do?'

'I told her about the wolves.'

'Oh no.'

'I didn't think she believed me.'

Innis remembered the conversation of the previous night. 'That's what she meant when she said the Barrens will save themselves. She thinks that if people know about the wolves then they'll never allow the wind turbines.'

'Which is probably true, but she doesn't understand. She never gave me the chance to explain why the wolves have to stay hidden.'

Innis looked at Lachlan in horror. 'Oh God. Kat's off to tell the world about the wild wolves of Nin.'

Lachlan's face twisted in despair. 'And we're stuck here. On the wrong side of the island!'

Chapter 34

Once again, Innis found himself clinging to the back of the quad bike as it barrelled along the narrow road towards town. Lachlan had the machine going full pelt and then some. As Innis held on for dear life, he had the ironic thought that Matt McGowan should be videoing this for his website.

They sped past the castle, past the track that led to his croft, past the point where the single-track road became two lanes. This only made Lachlan go faster, careering through town. He screeched to a stop beside the Harbour Hotel. The boys jumped from the quad bike, pulling off their helmets and hanging them over the machine.

'Are we too late?' Innis asked.

'I don't know.' Lachlan checked his phone again. 'She

still hasn't responded to my text.'

Innis moved to the hotel door, pulled it open and peered inside. The reception area was empty and quiet. 'What now?'

'Take a look inside.'

Innis stepped through the door and Lachlan followed, a few steps behind. Where was Kat? Had she spilt the beans already? Was Matt McGowan even now filming the wild wolves of Nin? Had the Geddes family's ancient pledge to keep the animals hidden been turned to dust?

He moved through the reception hall and one question at least was answered. In the small lounge area at the back, Matt was sitting in a tartan armchair, swiping his tablet. He looked up as he heard Innis approach.

'Innis, just the man.'

Innis looked around but couldn't see Kat. He was sighing with relief when a door banged behind him. He spun around to see the girl emerge from the ladies' loo.

'Hi Innis,' she said breezily.

Too late. They were much too late. He glanced at Lachlan and the boy looked angry and scared. Suddenly, Lachlan was the one who had brought an end to a promise kept for centuries, the one who had reneged on his royal duty.

'Your friend Katrina was offering some new footage for the website,' Matt said.

Innis felt sick. He had helped cause this, had brought

these people to the island, had brought the wolves out of their glen. The disaster that was to follow was on him.

'You can't do it,' he said quietly. 'You can't put it on your website.'

Matt McGowan gave a laugh. 'Of course I'm not going to put it on the website. Blowing up a wind turbine *would* be pretty dramatic. The best yet.' The man gave a rueful shake of the head at the thought. 'You can imagine the number of likes it would get. But I can't be seen to be encouraging illegal acts. Especially where children are involved. No, there will be no exploding wind turbines.' He pointed to Innis with the forefingers of both hands. 'Your leap is going to be the showstopper this week.'

Innis looked at Kat. 'It was just an idea,' she said with a half-smile. 'In case the leap was . . . less than successful.'

'So, are we all set for tomorrow?' Matt asked.

Innis nodded, waves of relief flooding over him. The wolves were safe, for now at least. 'Everything is ready. I'm ready.'

'The *world* is ready,' Matt said grandly. 'I've checked the weather forecast. It's not looking great. This storm is going to get worse.'

'I'll bring an umbrella,' Innis said.

'You can be like Mary Poppins and float across the gap,' said Kat.

'Bad weather will just add to the atmosphere,' Matt said. 'It'll increase the sense of danger.'

Innis shot a glance at Lachlan, whose shoulders were

slumped in relief. The vow had not been broken.

'We wouldn't want it to seem easy,' Innis said, stifling a smile and trying to look troubled. He suspected that Matt was holding out for a plunge rather than a leap. That wasn't going to happen, not now.

'Tomorrow morning we'll be on site nice and early to get set up. We'll have a countdown clock going on the website from midnight tonight. I've a bit of work to do on that just now. It's just a pity your internet is so bad. How people can live here I don't know.'

'The best things on our island can't be downloaded,' Kat said.

'I suppose. Anyway, the internet seems more reliable in my room, so I'm going to work from there.' The man lifted his tablet. 'I'll see you tonight. We'll chat and do some filming.'

'Tonight?' Innis said.

'At your pre-leap party. It seems the whole town is going to be there.'

'Oh aye, that,' Innis said hesitantly. *What pre-leap party?* he thought.

'Till tonight, then.' Matt McGowan disappeared up a narrow staircase.

Innis turned to Kat. 'You were going to blow up a wind turbine?'

'Of course not. That would be stupid. They haven't even been built yet.'

'Why are you here then?' demanded Lachlan.

'I came to tell Matt about your wolves. If there are wild wolves on Nin they'll never allow their habitat to be destroyed by a bunch of wind turbines.'

'But you didn't believe me.'

'And I'm still not convinced. But if the wolves *are* real then we'll need video to prove they exist. He's the guy with the proper camera gear.'

'You can't do that,' Lachlan said, desperation in his voice.

'But the wolves are absolutely our best bet for stopping the destruction of the Barrens.'

'So why didn't you tell?' Innis asked. 'Why the story about blowing up wind turbines?'

'I got your text message – thought I would hold off until you told me about this new plan.' She looked at the boys with an intensity bordering on scary. 'Whatever it is, it better work. Otherwise we're going back to my idea.'

'It's not a new plan as such,' Innis said. 'We've just made some changes to the original one.'

He explained Lachlan's idea of moving the location of the leap. The girl listened intently and said at the end, 'I suppose it might work. Couldn't you have thought of it days ago?'

Innis smiled sheepishly. 'Aye, it does seem kind of obvious.'

'Remember though, if it doesn't happen or something goes wrong I *will* tell the world about the wolves. No one would dare do anything to the Barrens if it was revealed that the place contained the hidden-for-centuries, last-remaining wild wolves of Scotland.' She pointed a finger at both boys and added, 'Though I will only truly believe in the wolves when I see one for myself.'

'So what now?' Innis asked. He turned to Lachlan.

'People are going to begin arriving on the afternoon ferry, so we have to act fast. We need to corral the wolves in their glen. Keep them out of sight.'

'And how do we do that?' Innis asked.

'Wolves can't resist a hunk of red meat. I was thinking we scatter a few sheep carcasses across the glen. There's a supply in a freezer back home. It'll keep them there for a day or two. That's all we need.'

'I'll come with you,' Innis said.

'You can't,' Kat said. 'You're needed here in Skulavaig.'

'Why?'

'We're throwing a party for you.'

Innis remembered Matt's earlier comments. 'Aye, what is this pre-leap party? I know nothing about it.'

'You weren't supposed to know about it. That Matt guy's an idiot.'

'But I hate surprise parties.'

'Well then, lucky for you it's no longer a surprise.' Kat looked him up and down. 'You'll need to get changed, you're soaked through.'

'I'll drop you off back home,' Lachlan said.

'You don't need a hand with the wolves?' Innis asked,

anxious to avoid the shindig.

'I can manage.' Lachlan turned to Kat. 'I'm sure we can fit three on the quad.'

'That's okay. I have to stay here and help set up for Innis's *no-longer-a-surprise* party.'

As he left the hotel, Innis looked out across the harbour and its solitary boat towards the ocean beyond. It was raining hard and the wind was picking up. Matt was right – there was a big storm coming. It felt like the winds of change were gusting already. Tomorrow was the day. Tomorrow was the leap. A day when he would do something momentous. On Nin, the islanders generally fell into two broad groups; those who wanted to stay and those who wanted to go. His mum was a goer. Gramps was a stayer. Kat was a goer, which was inevitable, since she wanted to be an astronaut. Innis had always thought that he was a goer as well, most young people were. Now, as he stood with his feet on the edge of his island, he realized *this* was as far as he wanted to go. He was a stayer. There was nothing out there across the water that called to him. Tomorrow, he was going to save his island and then he was going to stay on his island.

Why would he ever leave a place where birds flew high and wolves ran wild?

Chapter 35

I nnis had his head down and out of the rain, hanging
on to the quad as always, when Lachlan called out
over the noise of the engine.

'Dammit! Too soon.'

Innis looked up and saw people walking up the track
ahead. The strangers had just passed the crofts and were
climbing up on to the Barrens. Lachlan kept the quad
going and pulled up beside them. It was two boys and a
girl. They looked like uni students. Lachlan climbed off
the bike and Innis followed, pulling off his helmet. The
reaction was instant.

'You're the kid,' the girl said. 'You're Innis.'

'You're the Lord of the Leap,' one of the boys said.
'How cool is this.'

Innis nodded, embarrassed. 'Thanks.' He had waited

all his life for this moment, to be recognized and acclaimed by perfect strangers. Now that it was here, it felt hollow and awkward.

'What are you doing here?' the girl asked.

'This is where I live,' Innis said.

'Cooool,' said the second boy.

Lachlan asked in his old, unfriendly manner, 'Where are you going?'

'We just want a little look at the chasm,' the first boy said. 'Who are you?'

'None of your business. You're not allowed to go to the site.'

'Not yet,' Innis interjected. 'He means not yet. Not until tomorrow.'

'It's too far to walk anyway, especially in this weather,' Lachlan said.

'A little rain doesn't bother us,' said the girl.

Innis knew he had to keep people off the Barrens, at least until Lachlan had rounded up the wolves.

'Sorry, it's off-limits for now. Just in case someone decides . . . you know . . . to give it a go before me.' The three students looked disappointed. 'But if you head back to town you can join us tonight for a special pre-leap party in the Fishermen's Mission. Special invitation, just for you guys.'

'Awesome,' said one of the boys. The three strangers seemed satisfied and returned the way they had come.

'We need to work fast,' Lachlan said.

Innis exhaled a long breath. 'People are actually coming to watch me leap.'

'Of course they're coming. That website of yours has been inviting the world to come witness something amazing.'

'All I'm doing is jumping. Once. It's hardly entertaining.'

'Not exactly how the website is spinning it.'

'Aye.'

'History-making.'

Innis gave a mournful chuckle. 'Breath-taking.'

'Death-defying.'

'See a boy fly.'

'You'll be the newest member of the royal family.'

Innis shook his head in despair. 'I don't think the Laird of Nin gets to have breakfast with the Queen.'

The boys laughed for a moment, before their faces turned serious.

'This is really happening,' Innis said.

'It is. So we better get a move on. I still need to make sure the wolves are gathered in their glen.'

Innis shook his head in wonder. 'How do you know how to do all this stuff?'

'My uncle showed me. I shadowed him for weeks, learnt everything. He's been the sole guardian of the wolves for years.'

'And you're taking over?'

'That's the plan. Once I'm done with school.'

'I can help.'

'The best way you can help is becoming Laird of Nin.'

Innis nodded and tried to look confident. As the day and hour approached he could feel his nerves grow. 'Are you coming to the party later?'

'Maybe.' Lachlan climbed back on the quad and revved the engine. 'See you.'

It was then that Innis remembered.

'The carved stone! We haven't moved it yet.'

'I'll do it later, when I get back from the glen. Tomorrow we just point the crowd in the right direction.'

The quad bike roared away in a cloud of fumes and Innis looked out over the Barrens – now just shadows and silhouettes in the falling rain. This time tomorrow, all of it would belong to him. Either that, or he would be dead at the bottom of a cliff. He wiped a hand across his wet face, breathed deeply of the cool, clear air and wondered which of the two was the scarier.

Chapter 36

Innis felt another arm around his shoulder, looked up to see another camera pointing in his direction. Smile for the selfie.

'Best of luck for tomorrow,' said the stranger with the phone.

'Thanks,' Innis said. A photograph of himself was thrust in his hand. Another visitor in a hall full of them. Matt McGowan had produced some glossy pics for signing, promotion for the Graveheart tour. Innis signed his autograph and handed back the picture, getting a smile in return. A pretty girl in her twenties had smiled at him and asked for his autograph. Who would have imagined that a few weeks ago?

The Fishermen's Mission was full of affyerheid.com partygoers, all young, all here for a good time and a madcap stunt. The islanders in the hall were an older crowd; some gave disapproving looks and scrunched their faces at the loud music. In the midst of it all, Matt McGowan was filming everything.

Innis was trying to get to the door. He had grown tired of speeches reminding him how important his endeavour was to the future of the island. At first it had been fun – signing autographs and taking selfies – but the novelty had worn off. Only now, when it was all a little late, did Innis realize he didn't want this. He wasn't good in crowds. He didn't like attention. He had hoped for recognition, but when it came he realized he preferred anonymity. He just wanted to be left alone to leap.

Innis had reached the door of the Mission. Gramps was there, smoking a sly cigar.

'What are you doing?' Innis asked.

'I just needed some fresh air.'

Innis coughed. 'You won't get any smoking that thing.'

'One willnae do me harm.'

'That's not what the doctor says.'

Gramps tutted and asked, 'Where are you going?'

'There's too many people. It's all too much.'

'Aye, it's a good crowd. They're just here to wish you luck.'

'And drink whisky. There's a lot of that going on.'

Gramps chuckled. 'You need to get back inside. They've a little presentation to make.'

'I don't need trinkets. It's not why I'm doing it.'

His grandfather gave one of the kind, wise smiles that Innis loved. 'I know that, lad, but all these people have come to see you leap. And it makes the islanders feel good. They're worried for you.' Gramps placed a hand on his arm. 'We all are. You're doing something enormously dangerous tomorrow.'

'I'll be fine.'

'I'm sure of it.' There was a tremble in the man's voice. 'And I'm proud of you, lad.'

Innis felt his bottom lip quiver. 'Thanks.'

'If I didn't believe you could do it I would never have let you try. I know it's not just for Kat and her dark skies, I know it's not just to save the Barrens for the birds. I know you're doing it for me as well. That you're doing it for us.'

'If I'm Laird of Nin then we get to stay on the island.' He turned from his grandfather's kindly face. 'No matter what happens.'

Gramps smiled and squeezed his arm. 'Aye lad, aye.'

Innis wiped his watery eyes. 'I best get back in. They want a speech from me.'

His grandfather chuckled again. 'A few words of thanks will do.'

Innis stepped through the door and surveyed the shindig once more. Most of the island seemed to be here. And so many faces he didn't know. Kat's brothers were dancing with two pretty visitors. Mr Wallace, the harbour master, was standing in the corner tapping a foot. Dunny the silent boy was here with his parents and older brother. Only Innis's mother hadn't come. She'd said she couldn't watch. Innis was glad. He didn't want her there . . . just in case.

He moved into the room, was given a 'good luck' backslap by a stranger. One of his neighbours gave him a hug. He saw Matt McGowan heading his way for yet another online interview. Kat rescued him, pulling him halfway up the stairs to the harbour master's office. She had a look of concern on her face.

'Have you heard from Lachlan?' she asked.

'Isn't he here? He said he might come.'

'He's not, and he hasn't replied to my text.'

Innis shrugged. 'He must still be rounding up the last of the wolves.'

'But it's dark out there.'

'Wolves are nocturnal. I think Lachlan is as well.'

'I'm worried about him.'

'He probably didn't fancy the party. I can't blame him.'

'At least pretend you're having fun.'

'I thought I was.'

Kat sighed. 'And you're sure everything is ready for tomorrow.'

'I'm sure. And don't worry, I can make it across the new gap. It will only be cheating a wee bit.'

Kat smiled and turned to head back down the stairs.

'Wait,' Innis said. 'I need to say something.' The girl stopped and looked up at him. 'If – if things go wrong tomorrow.'

'But you said you can make it.'

'I can, but just on the off chance that I don't, you need to promise me something.'

'What?'

'No more sabotage or vandalism. You'll ruin your future. I don't think NASA employs criminals.'

Kat looked at him in dismay. 'You can't still think I'm responsible?'

'You were going to blow up a wind turbine.'

'I wasn't being serious. I had to say something.'

'Tell me you hadn't considered it at all.'

From the evasive look on her face, Innis could tell an explosion had been contemplated.

'I am not the saboteur,' she said.

'Who is then?'

'You really have no idea?'

'No. Do you?' Innis saw a flicker in Kat's face, a narrowing of the eyes. She did know. 'You do know. Tell me.'

'I can't.'

'You have to.'

'I won't.'

'Who is it?'

Kat had a pained look on her face, as if her heart was tearing at the edges. 'I'm going back to the party.'

'Is it Lachlan? Was it him all along?' Kat walked

quickly down the stairs. 'Were you helping him? Did he ask you to set fire to the truck?'

Kat was gone. Innis waited a few moments then returned to the loud music and louder people. He saw his grandfather lift a whisky glass to his lips with a trembling hand. He wasn't supposed to drink alcohol either. There was too much laughter in the room, too much merriment. Tomorrow there was a chance he could die and people were partying. Surely a sombre, silent vigil was more appropriate?

Innis spun on his heels and headed for the door. He burst from the building into a strong wind filled with falling rain. He didn't look back as he marched off in the direction of home.

Chapter 37

The Big Day had arrived. Innis stood in the doorway of the croft and watched raindrops scatter in the strong wind. With the day had come the storm.

'Morning, lad.'

He turned to see his grandfather. The man was having difficulty pulling on his dressing gown. Innis closed the front door and went over to help.

'Thanks,' said Gramps, 'I'm a little under the weather this morning.'

'You've a hangover, is what you mean. You know you're not supposed to drink.'

'It was a special occasion. I had to toast my own grandson.'

Innis rolled his eyes and moved to the sink to fill the kettle. 'Sorry I disappeared last night. It was all getting a bit much.'

'Dinnae worry about that. I said you had to get home and rest. Tired legs willnae fly.' The old man chortled at his own joke. 'People understood. Although that film director laddie wasnae too pleased.'

'Oh, I think he got enough from me.'

'I accepted something on your behalf. It's over there.'

Innis looked towards the fire. On the mantelpiece sat a carved piece of glass. He moved to have a closer look.

'It's crystal,' his grandfather said.

It was a twinkling bird in flight and on the base there was an engraving:

To Innis Munro, Lord of the Leap. From the people of Nin.

'I'm not Lord yet,' Innis said.

Now he felt bad. He had stormed away in a huff when the islanders were doing a kind thing for him. He smiled bleakly at the thought that most of them would be there this afternoon. He could thank every one of them in person. If he survived.

'It's nice.'

'Aye.' Gramps collapsed into the big chair beside the fireplace and began to prod the cold ashes with a poker.

'I'll sort the fire.'

'I can manage. You get the tea going.' Innis returned to the kettle and Gramps asked, 'So when is the big event?'

His grandfather had forgotten already. Another sign that the Parkinson's was progressing. The hour had been announced several times during the party. 'It's not until two o'clock.'

'Why wait so long?'

'The website is showing the leap live, so they want to wait until American viewers might be awake. They wanted to do it even later but I told them it might be dark by three.'

'What are your plans in the meantime?'

'I'm going to lie low. It'll be a circus as it is – might as well delay for as long as possible.'

'Good idea. A big breakfast, a restful morning, a light lunch and you'll be good to go.'

'I hope so. What are your plans?'

'I'll get a ride to the leap later with the McColls.'

'Are you sure you want to be there?'

'I wouldnae miss it for the world. I want to see my grandson stand on the other side of the gap as the new Laird of Nin.'

Innis imagined the triumphant moment and it gave him a little tingle. He reached for a pan. 'And when I'm Laird of Nin, someone else can scramble our eggs.'

After breakfast, Innis showered and dressed then lay on his bed and tried unsuccessfully to relax. He took a call from Matt McGowan, who was seeking reassurance that he was ready to leap. He read and responded to messages from classmates, either wishing him luck or reminding him that today was the day he died. The two people he didn't hear from all morning were Kat and Lachlan. He wished he hadn't argued with Kat. He needed her support today. He assumed Lachlan was doing some last-minute sorting.

At midday, Innis lifted himself from his bed and turned off his music. Two hours to go. He walked into the living room and found his grandfather sitting by the fire. He thought he was dozing, but Gramps roused himself and said, 'Not long now. How are you holding up?'

'Fine. I just want to get on with it.'

Innis's phone buzzed once more. It was getting tiring but he always had to look. It was a message from Lachlan. At last! Innis had been trying all morning to get in touch.

The message said, *Stuck on ledge. Need help.*

What did that mean exactly? Innis replied, *Where r u?*

There was no response. As Innis was composing another text, the door opened and Kat marched in. She was also looking at her phone.

'Have you heard from Lachlan?' she asked.

'I've just had a message from him.'

'What does it say?'

Innis looked again to get the wording right. 'Stuck on ledge. Need help.'

'That's the same message I got.'

'I've tried to reply but I'm getting nothing back.'

'What ledge?' Kat asked.

Suddenly, Innis knew. He had been on it himself. 'It must be the one on the cliff face. The one by the castle.

It leads to the wolf cave.'

He saw Kat's doubting face but focused on finding his jacket and boots. He pulled them on quickly and stepped out into the rain. Kat followed.

'Best of luck. Dinnae be late for the leap,' Gramps called after them.

Innis headed towards the coast and jogged up the path that ran along the clifftop. He could see the castle in the distance. Rain was battering the ground and wind was gusting across the high cliff. Kat caught up and bent her body into the weather. Lachlan's quad bike sat on the grass.

'He was here,' Innis said.

He inched towards the edge and looked over. He felt Kat grab on to his jacket. Below him, the ledge moved down the cliff face and disappeared around the curve of the rock. There was no sign of Lachlan.

'There *is* a ledge,' Kat said.

'Told you.'

'You're not going down there?'

'We have to.'

'We?'

'You can't be an astronaut and be afraid of heights.'

'I'm not afraid of heights. No one is afraid of heights. It's gravity that should scare you. That's what kills you. There's no gravity in space.'

'So are you coming or not?'

'Aye, I'm coming.'

Innis lowered himself carefully down on to the ledge before helping Kat down. In the shelter of the cliff face the wind was not as gusting, although the rain still fell in sheets. Innis began edging his way along the rocky shelf, not looking down. The stone ledge had moss and tufts of grass growing on it and was becoming slick as rainwater ran down its slope.

Innis moved slowly down the ledge towards the cave and reached the point where the cliff curved. Here, the shelf was narrower. He pressed his back to the rock and focused on the ocean far in the distance. His feet shuffled slowly until he was around the curve and when he looked ahead, there sat Lachlan Geddes. The boy was side on, squeezed against the rock wall, his legs pulled tight to his chest, shivering hard.

'Lachlan!' Innis shouted as he began to move quickly towards him.

'Stop!' Lachlan screamed. 'Stop right there!'

Innis skidded to a halt and Kat banged into him from behind. Lachlan raised himself slowly to his feet. 'Come no further.'

Innis looked and saw the reason why. The rock ledge between himself and Lachlan was gone. A large section had crumbled away and fallen to the beach below.

'What happened?' Innis asked, although it was painfully obvious.

'I'm trapped. The ledge collapsed behind me as I walked along it.'

'Are you okay where you are?' Kat asked.

'This bit's more solid. I've been here all night. I'm very cold and very wet.'

'Why did you not shelter in the cave?' Innis asked. 'Why not get back out through the castle?'

'The bit of ledge in front of me is full of cracks. I thought that bit might collapse as well if I stood on it.' Lachlan pushed his body flat against the cliff face. 'I'm trapped on this one wee section. I don't know how much longer it will last. It might crumble any minute.'

And in that moment there seemed to be the very real possibility that *two* boys might fall to their death this day from the high cliffs of Nin.

Chapter 38

'What should we do?' Innis asked.

Lachlan was rubbing his body, trying to get the blood flowing again. 'We need something to bridge the gap. A plank of wood or something.'

Kat said, 'My dad has a long ladder. That might work.'

'Can you bring it here? It has to be just the two of you, no one else.'

'We can manage.' Now it was Kat in charge. 'We'll be back soon.'

Kat and Innis scurried carefully back along the ledge. Innis looked down with every step – if that part of the ledge could collapse, why not this bit? He only breathed properly when they had climbed back on to the clifftop. They dashed through the driving rain to Kat's croft.

Skirting past the house, watchful for older brothers, they reached the stone shed that housed tools and dad junk. Lying against the back wall was an old wooden ladder.

'This will be hard to do without anyone seeing us,' Innis said in a whisper.

'We move fast and hope no one is looking.'

They each lifted an end of the ladder and hurried along the edge of the moor, away from the track. Innis kept an eye on the house windows but didn't see anyone looking out. When they were beyond the crofts they angled back towards the coast, panting hard as they sprinted. At the cliff edge they paused for breath.

'How do we do this?' Innis asked.

'Very carefully.'

He eased down on to the ledge and Kat let down the ladder. Innis leant it against the wall and held on tight while the wind tried to blow it over the drop. Kat lowered herself on to the ledge and with Innis in front and her behind they once again shuffled back towards the spot where they had left Lachlan. It was harder to balance carrying the ladder and they had increased the weight resting on a fragile shelf of crumbly rock. Innis tried not to think about it.

'Well done,' Lachlan said when they arrived back at the fractured ledge.

The ladder was lowered to the ground and slowly slid across the gap. Lachlan crouched down and waited to receive it.

'You could have jumped this gap,' Innis said. 'It's narrower than mine.'

'I was going to,' Lachlan said, 'but I was worried the whole ledge would break off when I landed.'

The boy straightened himself up, pressed a few times with his foot on the end of the ladder.

'Right then, let's hope it holds.'

Kat was about to say something, a word of warning or encouragement, but Lachlan took off without a second's hesitation, stepping carefully from rung to rung as if he was tiptoeing through a puddle. The ladder held and he made it to the other side, collapsing in the arms of Innis.

'Oh thank goodness,' Kat said.

Innis hoisted the boy up straight, felt a tremble in Lachlan's body. Lachlan was mortal like the rest of them, and felt fear just the same.

'You've been here all night?' Kat asked.

'I have. I'll explain once we get off this ledge.'

The three of them walked back along the rock shelf, carrying the ladder and keeping a gap between each other so there wasn't too much weight on any one spot. They climbed back to the top of the cliff and stood on the wet grass, catching their breath and enjoying the reassurance of solid rock beneath them.

'So, what happened? Innis asked.

Lachlan shook his head and sighed, as if even he found it hard to believe. 'All the wolves were safely corralled in the glen, but I thought I should do one last check of the cave, just in case I'd missed one. As I walked along the ledge the whole thing collapsed behind me. It's all this rain we've been having, it's weakened the rock.'

'It's lucky the whole thing didn't collapse.'

'Very lucky. Anyway, I wasn't worried at that point because I knew I could get out through the cave and passageway. But then I noticed the rock in front was full of cracks. I couldn't risk it. So that was me, stuck on the ledge. I was there all night, trying not to fall asleep and roll off the edge.'

'Why didn't you phone?' Kat asked.

'I tried. But with the cliff face right there it blocked any kind of signal. This morning I shouted and waited for someone to come but no one did. Then the idea came to try something. If that didn't work I was going to have to jump the gap.'

'What did you do?' Kat asked.

'I wrote a text message to you both. I made it short in case long messages took more time to send. Then I tossed my phone as high and as far from the cliff as I could in the hope that as it fell it might make contact with a mast or satellite and send the texts.'

'We got your message,' Kat said.

Lachlan shook his head in disbelief. 'I'm amazed it worked.'

'We should go down and fetch your phone,' Innis said.

Lachlan laughed. 'No point, it'll either be washed out

to sea or broken into pieces.'

'We don't have time anyway,' Kat said. She turned to Innis. 'You need to be over on the other side of the island.'

'After what we've just done, the leap will be the easy bit.'

Innis laughed and Kat laughed but Lachlan stood with a look of shock on his face.

'Oh my God,' he said. 'The stone. The stone that marks the Bonnie Laddie's Leap.'

'What about it?' Kat asked.

Innis knew already. It made his legs go weak and he thought he was going to be sick.

'I've been stuck here all night,' Lachlan said, aghast. 'I never got the chance to move the stone from its original site to the new one.'

Innis glanced at the time on his phone, saw it was after one. People would be gathering to watch him leap. Matt McGowan would be getting set up.

He said with a strangled moan, 'They'll be there by now. They'll be at the original site. The one that's too wide to cross. They'll be waiting to see me leap.'

The cunning plan had fallen apart. They were back to the first idea, the first chasm. The one where he would plummet on to wave-smacked rocks. Innis's legs buckled and he sank to his knees, clutching at the grass as if he was falling to his doom already.

Chapter 39

'Everyone's here,' Lachlan said quietly.

It was just before two. The wildlife sanctuary was full of people. There were a dozen vehicles parked at the end of the track, including Kat's family Land Rover. Beyond the buildings, they could see figures milling around or standing in the shelter of walls, trying to get out of the relentless rain.

'They've come,' Kat said.

'What now?' Lachlan asked.

From the distance, from out across the sea, came a low rumble of thunder. Innis began walking. He had no idea *what now*. People had come to see him leap. The moment had arrived. Already folk were turning in his direction, were recognizing him. He heard an excited babble of voices and bodies began closing in. Someone cheered, someone shouted, someone grabbed his arm. Innis turned his head to look. It felt like he was underwater, everything seemed to be slower, to be hazy. It was Matt McGowan.

'Where have you been?'

Innis noticed another cameraman, filming everything.

'I'm here on time.'

'Only just.'

'Well, I'm here.'

'There's a lot riding on this.'

'I know.' Innis's lot was not the same as Matt's lot. What Innis had riding on this was life itself.

'Everything's set up. We'll get a tracking shot first and then go close . . .'

Innis walked on, left Matt to be swallowed by the crowd that was now following him. He moved past the buildings and there was the cliff edge, waiting for him. Another rumble of thunder came, closer. The sky was dark; full of black, churning clouds. There were a lot of people here, hundreds maybe. All come to see him leap. Some he recognized as islanders, some were faces he had never seen before. The faces all wore the same expression of eager anticipation. Innis suddenly had an image of a gladiator entering the Colosseum of Rome. That was what it felt like. They were here for a show. They were here for blood.

'Are you sure about this, lad?'

It was Gramps speaking. *His* face showed only deep

concern. Innis pushed back a sob. He had an over-whelming urge to cling to his grandfather and bury his face and block out these people, this place. Instead, he gave a smile and repeated his mantra.

'It'll be fine.'

'I've had a look lad. It seems awfy far. It looks more than two metres.'

'It's okay. It will all be okay.'

The people were standing in two lines now, forming a path that led to the start of the run-up. Innis moved around in a circle. So many people. Matt was filming. Lachlan and his uncle looked wretched. Gramps looked fearful. There was no sign of Kat. He progressed along the path as if propelled by a force not under his control. The cheers were just a dull noise that merged with his heavy breaths, trembling in and out. The sky was lit by a brief flash of lightning, out to sea but not too far. Thunder rumbled soon after.

Innis reached the edge of the cliff and looked along the path he was to run. It was lined by people, every head peering in his direction. A chant began.

In-nis, In-nis, In-nis, In-nis, In-nis, In-nis . . .

There was another flash of lightning with a simulta-neous clap of thunder. The crowd went *oooh*. And there was Kat in the light, her hand raised. He couldn't hear what she was saying but her lips seemed to mouth, *don't do this*. Innis could hear only the boom of waves hurling themselves against the cliff.

The chant started up once more. Innis looked again along the path, could see the point where the chasm began, where there was only air and a drop to the rocks below.

This was it.

All that had gone on in the weeks before had been leading to this moment in time. Every road he had walked had been leading to this place. The Bonnie Laddie's Leap was waiting to be leapt.

He knew he would never make it.

But he couldn't back out now.

Could he?

The welfare of his grandfather depended on it. The expectations of an island rested on him. The world was watching.

But he would never make it.

Would he?

In-nis, In-nis, In-nis, In-nis, In-nis, In-nis . . .

He turned to his grandfather, who was standing behind him.

'What do I do?'

Gramps smiled his wise, kind smile. 'You do your best lad. That's all you can do.'

Innis had wanted this so badly and now he had it, every single bit of it. Even if he wished to, he couldn't walk away. He peeled off his wet jacket. He had intended to wear his running shoes and shorts, but here he stood in his jeans and boots. It didn't matter. He tried to focus, tried to remember his training, but it was all a blur. It didn't matter. He would run fast. He would leap. And then he would land. Somewhere.

Innis pressed his feet into the ground and bent his knees. He lifted his head and focused on the point where he would have to launch. He took three deep breaths to fill his lungs. On the next breath, he would run.

Chapter 40

Another flash of lightning illuminated the clifftop, so close that the air seemed to spark. Innis felt his body prickle and his hair stand on end. The thunder that followed a second later was loud enough to shake the sky. People on the clifftop ducked down, others screamed. For a few moments, the air felt charged. The chanting had come to a stop. Everyone was watching the sky now. A ripple of panic passed through the crowd.

Innis tried to focus, but the attention was no longer on him. There was a scream, the crowd parted, another scream and then a shout.

'That's a wolf!'

Innis turned and saw the big black wolf. It was running among the crowd, brushing their legs and weaving between them. People were fleeing in panic, falling over themselves to get away. The wolf ran the length of the cliff as if *it* was about to leap, scattering people like skittles. It stopped at the edge and turned. Another flash of lightning tore open the dark and electricity shimmered across the clifftop. The wolf raised its head and howled.

Innis was the only one who hadn't moved. People were running in confused panic. The wolf came back towards him. Another sustained burst of lightning lit the sky and the wolf stopped in front of Innis. For a moment, in the brightness, Innis looked at the wolf and the wolf looked back and an understanding of sorts passed between them. The animal was big, its head was higher than Innis's waist and he reached down to stroke the black fur above its piercing yellow eyes. And then it was dark again. The wolf ran past him and was gone.

'Get off this cliff!' shouted a voice. Innis looked and saw a policeman waving the crowd away. People were fleeing. Where had the policeman come from? Innis turned the other way and saw Lachlan standing with Kat, bodies rushing past them. His friends seemed frozen, unsure what to do. He turned again, looking for Gramps.

And there stood his grandfather, another policeman holding his arm.

Innis moved quickly towards them but the first policeman grabbed him and said, 'Get under cover, before you're struck by lightning.'

Innis pointed. 'My grandfather.'

The policeman hauled Innis with him and they caught up with Gramps, who was being led to safety by the other officer. They stepped inside the building that had cages and hay bales and other equipment.

'Bloody hell,' said the first policeman.

Another rumble of thunder rattled the roof.

'What were you all doing out there?' the second policeman asked.

The first policeman answered. 'It's that leap thing today.' The man shook his head. 'Did you not check the weather forecast?'

Lachlan's uncle entered the building. 'It's okay now, the cliff is clear. People are sheltering in various buildings or in their cars. We'll move them on when the storm passes.'

'Why are you here?' Innis asked the policemen. 'Did someone ask you to come?'

'We're looking for John McGarrah,' said one. 'We were told we would find him out here.'

Gramps said, 'I'm the one you seek.'

The policemen looked first at Gramps and then at each other, eyes wide with surprise. They had clearly not been expecting an old man.

'Your name has come up in an investigation. We've been looking into the sabotage and vandalism that's been occurring on the island.'

Gramps snorted. 'Why does everyone keep calling it

sabotage? It's hardly sabotage.'

'So you are involved?'

Innis stepped forwards. 'Of course he's not involved. My grandfather is old. And he's not well. He has Parkinson's disease.'

'Is this true?' the policeman asked, as if he couldn't take the word of a thirteen-year-old boy.

Gramps lifted both arms and his hands had a tremble.

'Why are you interrogating my neighbour?' It was Kat's mum. 'Can't you see he's very frail?'

Kat stood beside her. Like everyone else, they were drenched and bedraggled.

The policemen stood in silence for a moment and then one said, 'Sorry, we were misinformed.' He turned to Gramps. 'Sorry to trouble you, sir.'

'That's quite all right officer. You're just doing your job.'

Kat's mum said, 'Let's get you home and out of those wet clothes.'

'A cup of tea would be nice.'

The policemen touched their caps and departed. Gramps watched them go and gave Innis a wink.

'Are you okay?' Innis asked.

'I'm fine.' He placed a hand on Innis's arm. 'Sorry about your leap lad. Probably for the best.'

'Aye. Never mind.' Innis took a long look at his grandfather. He asked quietly, 'Why did those policemen want to speak to you?'

Kat's mum was gathering up wet things. 'Are you two coming?' she asked.

'We'll be there in a minute, lass,' said Gramps.

Innis waited a moment until it was just him and his grandfather. '*Is* it you who has been doing the sabotage?'

Gramps gave a laugh. 'Who started calling it sabotage? Sabotage in my day was blowing up bridges and derailing trains.' He laughed again, and then his face turned serious. 'I expected this question a week ago.'

'So it *is* you?'

His grandfather sighed. 'Aye lad. But sabotage is a little grand. Let's call it small acts of mischief. I never destroyed anything, never hurt anyone.'

Innis was stunned. It was his grandfather. It wasn't Lachlan. It wasn't Kat. It was Gramps all along. 'What about the pickup truck that caught fire?'

'That wasnae me. That was those security laddies. I dinnae ken what they did but they blamed the *saboteur* to cover their own backs.'

There was another clap of thunder but this one was further away, beyond them.

'But how did you do it? Your illness. You haven't the strength.'

'You find the strength when protecting something you love.'

'Is that *why* you did it?'

'I was trying to make life difficult for the people

ruining the Barrens with their metal monstrosities. I understand we need wind power, but the Barrens just isnae the place for it. I was trying to get the message home that they werenae wanted.' Gramps paused and when he spoke again his voice was quieter. 'I wanted to do something while I still had the strength. I know it willnae be long before that's gone completely, before I'm no use to anyone any more.'

'That will never happen.'

His grandfather gave a sad smile. 'Thanks, lad.'

'But you have to stop your . . . small acts of mischief. Eventually you'll be discovered.'

'Aye, the moment has passed. It had no effect. They're building on the Barrens regardless. That's why your leap was so important.'

'I'm sorry. I'm sorry I never tried.'

'No. It's for the best.' Gramps gave Innis a final heartening squeeze of the arm. 'The wind wasnae at your back today.'

Innis and his grandfather walked to the Land Rover. The storm was passing and the rain had lessened, though still it fell. In the distance, over the ocean, the sky had a brightness that had been missing all day. Cars were leaving and some people were walking on foot down the track. Innis helped his grandfather into the car.

'Are you coming?' Kat's mum asked.

'Not yet,' Innis said.

'I'll stay for a bit as well,' said Kat.

Innis and Kat waved them away. They saw Matt McGowan loading up his equipment. Innis walked over to him.

'Sorry the leap never happened.'

Innis expected Matt to be angry, but he simply shrugged.

'Not your fault. Anyway, that was wild. It was better than wild, it was spectacular. All that lightning. All the people running. And we got some footage of the wolf. You touched a wolf, my friend. Spectacular. It's going viral already.'

'What about the leap?'

'Don't worry about that. We'll do it next time we're up this way.'

'You don't want your money back?'

Matt laughed. 'I think we got our money's worth.'

Innis watched them leave and then everyone was gone and he and Kat walked in silence back to the buildings. Lachlan was waiting for them.

'Everyone saw the wolf,' Innis said.

'I know,' said Lachlan. 'It was pretty incredible.' He turned to Kat. '*Now* do you believe?'

She nodded. 'I do. And I'm sorry I ever thought about exposing them. That wolf was completely . . .' She tailed off.

'Why was it here?' Innis asked

Lachlan gave his enigmatic smile. 'I think it came to save you.'

'Save me from what?'

'From yourself. From doing an impossible leap.'

'Just like the wolves saved Bonnie Prince Charlie,' Kat said.

'Exactly.'

'No way,' said Innis, but he smiled and liked the idea of it. 'The wolf was filmed. People will know.'

'We'll say it escaped from the wildlife sanctuary. That a fence blew down in the storm.'

Innis nodded. It was a reasonable explanation if anyone asked. Not that it mattered any more. He had failed in his quest to be Laird of Nin. The turbines were coming and perhaps the discovery of the wolves was inevitable now. He sighed and turned and walked back towards the cliff.

'Where are you going?' Kat asked.

'For a last look.'

He reached the cliff edge and moved along the path he had been planning to run. Would he really have attempted the leap? Innis thought back and didn't know. He stood where the land fell away and the chasm began, looked down at the crashing waves. It was a scarily long way to the other side. He sensed Kat and Lachlan behind him.

'I could just go for it now,' he said.

'We'll have to fish out your body before the tide turns,' said Lachlan.

'I might have made it.'

'And I might be the first person to step foot on Mars,' Kat said.

Innis gave her his most forceful look. 'Yes, you will be. You absolutely will be.'

In silence, they contemplated the gap that had only ever been crossed once, by the Bonnie Laddie himself. The redcoat soldiers at his heels, his desperate leap, his pursuers scattered by black wolves risen from the shadows.

Or so the legend said.

Chapter 41

Innis sat on the low wall of Kat's garden, watching her watching the stars. He wondered how many nights like this she had left.

'It's been quite a day,' he said.

'This is the best way to end it.'

'So you knew it was Gramps all along?'

'I didn't know, I just suspected. I saw him one night, out on the Barrens by himself.'

'Why didn't you tell me?'

'Unlike some, I didn't want to make accusations before I had proof.'

'Okay, I said I'm sorry.'

'And I'll want to hear it a few more times.'

The girl returned to her telescope and Innis smiled to himself. He had been forgiven.

'What are you looking at?' he asked after a while.

Kat lifted her face from the eyepiece. 'Come and see.'

Innis jumped from the wall and moved to the telescope, bent down and had a look.

'Your favourite.'

Kat had focused on the moon, and it was as if Innis was looking down on it from a high hill. He could see every crater spread across its grey surface. If he looked hard enough, he thought he might see a footprint in the moondust.

'It was so bright tonight and so close,' Kat said, 'It would be rude not to admire it. One day I shall stand upon its surface.'

Innis stepped away from the telescope. 'You know, whatever happens here on the island, the moon will still be there, the stars will still be there.'

'I know. But I might have to leave to see them better.'

'I think you were always going to do that anyway.'

'And no matter what,' the girl said, 'the island will still be here for you. It's in your name.'

'I know, Innis means island.'

'More than that. Rearrange the letters.'

'How do you mean?'

'Innis. Nin is. Nin is Innis.'

The boy laughed and said, 'I never saw that before.'

They both turned at the sound of a vehicle. Innis looked at his phone and wondered who was driving up their track at ten o'clock. Headlights shone across the crofts as both Innis and Kat moved towards the road. It was the pickup truck that belonged to Dougal Geddes. It pulled up beside Kat's croft. The passenger window rolled down and Lachlan's head popped out.

'Get in,' he said. 'Both of you.'

'Why?' asked Innis.

'There's something you need to see.'

'What?'

Lachlan smiled his inscrutable smile. 'Just come.'

Innis and Kat climbed in the back and Lachlan's uncle drove them to the wildlife sanctuary. On the way, Lachlan refused to say any more, sharing an amused glance with his uncle now and again. Kat sent her mum a text and asked her to look in on Gramps, let him know where they'd gone.

They parked at the end of the track and all four piled out. Dougal Geddes headed for the croft, saying only, 'You folks have fun.'

'What's going on, Lachlan?' Kat asked.

That smile again. 'Come, and I'll show you.'

He led the two of them back towards the cliff. Innis thought it strange that he should be back here already, when he had sworn to himself never to return.

When they reached the path, Lachlan said, 'It happened about an hour ago. We heard this roar and then a boom. We came to look, saw this.'

He walked along the cliff edge towards the site of the leap, stopped and pointed.

'What's happened?' Kat asked, her eyes widening.

'It's all the rain we've had. It weakened the rock. The cliff has slumped on both sides.'

Innis stared and his jaw dropped in wonder. The path up to the launch point had lost a third of its distance. The end portion fell away, sloping down and then flattening out beneath the clifftop. The cliff on the other side had collapsed in a similar manner. The spot where he would have landed had slumped towards the sea. The two sides at the top were further apart, but part-way down, the falling rock and earth had slid out into the gap on both sides. There, it had heaped together. It meant that the chasm was now narrower lower down, only half the distance it had been.

'You could get down there,' Lachlan said. 'And then jump.'

'Do you see what this means?' Kat said.

Innis gave a disbelieving laugh. 'The Bonnie Laddie's Leap is not nearly as wide as it was.'

'You slide down the slope and then there's a flat bit to run and then you launch yourself,' said Lachlan.

'It's still a good gap. And it's still a long drop down to the water and the rocks.'

'If it wasn't a challenge it wouldn't be worth doing.'

'Do you think it still counts?' Kat asked.

'I don't see why not,' said Innis. 'It's still the same cleft in the same cliff. It's still the Bonnie Laddie's Leap.'

'So what's stopping you?' asked Lachlan.

What *was* stopping him? It was clear what he had to do. As clear and bright as the moon shining above his head. *This* was his moment. Innis pulled his phone from his pocket and handed it to Kat.

'Film it. Otherwise no one will believe us.'

'Are you really going to do this?' she asked.

'I really am.'

'That fall will still kill you.'

'I don't intend to fall. I intend to leap.'

Innis stepped up to the edge and took a close look at what lay below. The glimmering moon allowed him to see the run-up, now more of a run-*down* where the cliff had slumped. He could see where the ground flattened out and provided a short platform to launch himself. He could also see where he might land on the other side. The moonbeams illuminated the rolling ocean far below. The jagged rocks were still there, waves breaking over them just as his body would break if he got it wrong. The gap had narrowed but it would still take his best ever leap to make it to the other side.

'Are you sure about this, Innis?' Kat asked, a tremble in her voice.

'This is what I'm meant to do.'

'It is,' said Lachlan. 'Look.'

He pointed across to the other side of the cliff. At the top stood three black wolves. The big one raised it's head to the moon and howled and the other two followed, their calls echoing down through the chasm and out over the ocean.

It was the most thrilling sound Innis had ever heard. The wolves had chosen.

He took a few steps back and took a few deep breaths. He focused on the point ahead, where he would have to fly for a few quick heartbeats. His world had shrunk to this tiny piece of rock on a small island at the edge of the world. The moon shone to light his way, he felt the wind at his back to push him on. All that had happened in the last few weeks had been leading to these next few seconds.

Innis took a breath and ran. The ground sloped down and he felt himself slide as much as sprint but he dug his feet into the soil and pumped his legs and pushed himself forwards with every bit of his strength. He heard Lachlan yell, 'Go on!' heard Kat scream, 'Fly, Innis, fly!' The ground levelled out and there were only three more steps and then he was at the edge and he planted his foot and drove off with everything he had.

He was in the air. It was quiet now. He looked up and saw the stars, looked down and saw the sea. He had waited a long time to be in this place, free from the earth, one with the wind, an eagle at last. For a moment, he hoped he would never come down. And then he was falling, falling, falling . . .

He landed hard and his legs buckled and he fell forwards, arms outstretched, hands driving into wet soil. His face hit the ground, he slid through mud, twisted round, rolled over and came to a stop.

All was still. He lay with his eyes closed, waiting for the pain or the death throes, but nothing happened. He opened his eyes and looked at the twinkling stars high above him. Slowly he sat up, took in his surroundings, saw that he was on the solid ground of the other side of chasm. He lifted himself to his feet. On the cliff above stood Kat and Lachlan, jumping and cheering.

Innis stood and contemplated exactly what he had just achieved. He had crossed the Bonnie Laddie's Leap. He raised his arms in triumph and shouted to the moon above and the ocean below.

'I am Innis Munro, thirteenth Laird of the Island of Nin!'

He moved in a slow circle, took in the imaginary applause of a world that was no longer watching. It didn't matter. It didn't matter one little bit. He shouted again at the top of his voice.

'I am Innis Munro, Lord of the Leap!'

From somewhere high above him came the answering howl of a wolf.

Acknowledgements

My heartfelt thanks first of all to my family; Susan, Samuel and Jessica, who indulge me and encourage me and inspire me every day.

My grateful thanks also to my publisher Barry Cunningham who loves children's books and loves Scotland and so luckily for me will take a chance on children's books set in Scotland!

My indebted thanks to my wonderful editor Rachel Leyshon who is able every time to find the heart of a book and gently nudge me in that direction.

And final thanks to Rachel Hickman, Elinor Bagenal and the rest of the team at Chicken House. What a great job you do and what a publishing house you have created.

TRY ANOTHER GREAT BOOK FROM CHICKEN HOUSE

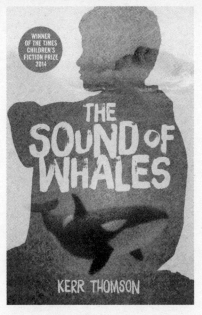

THE SOUND OF WHALES by KERR THOMSON

On a wild Scottish island, a tragedy washes up on the storm-beaten shore: the bodies of a whale and a man. Fraser, desperate for adventure, and American visitor Hayley, fed up with the island's isolation, become tangled up in the mystery.

But Fraser's younger brother Dunny is distraught by the discovery. He hasn't spoken in years, and lately he's been acting more strangely than ever. The whispering sea conceals a terrible secret. To discover the truth, someone must learn to listen . . .

WINNER OF THE *TIMES*/CHICKEN HOUSE CHILDREN'S FICTION COMPETITION 2014

'I was gripped . . . There aren't enough good modern novels that explore children's relationships with animals and nature. Thomson's ambitious plot, tight, poetic prose and feel for history is a breath of island air.'
THE TIMES

Paperback, ISBN 978-1-910002-27-8, £6.99 • ebook, ISBN 978-1-910002-28-5, £6.99

TRY ANOTHER GREAT BOOK FROM CHICKEN HOUSE

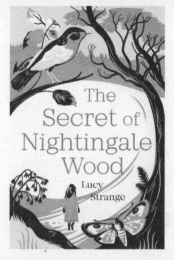

THE SECRET OF NIGHTINGALE WOOD
by LUCY STRANGE

Something terrible has happened in the Abbott family and nobody is talking about it.

Mama is ill. Father has taken a job abroad. Nanny Jane is too busy looking after baby Piglet to pay any attention to Henrietta and the things she sees – or thinks she sees – in the shadows of their new home, Hope House.

All alone, with only stories for company, Henry discovers that Hope House is full of strange secrets: a forgotten attic, thick with cobwebs; ghostly figures glimpsed through dusty windows; mysterious firelight that flickers in the trees beyond the garden.

One night she ventures into the darkness of Nightingale Wood. What she finds there will change her whole world . . .

'Superbly balanced between readability and poetry [...] this is an assured debut.'
GUARDIAN

'Perfect in so many ways!'
EMMA CARROLL

Paperback, ISBN 978-1-910655-03-0, £6.99 • ebook, ISBN 978-1-910655-63-4, £6.99

TRY ANOTHER GREAT BOOK FROM CHICKEN HOUSE

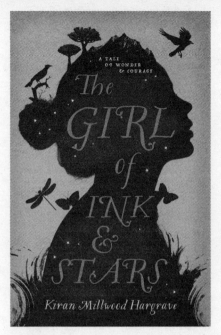

THE GIRL OF INK & STARS
by KIRAN MILLWOOD HARGRAVE

Forbidden to leave her island, Isabella dreams of the faraway lands her father once mapped. When her best friend disappears, she's determined to be part of the search party. Guided by an ancient map and her knowledge of the stars, Isabella navigates the island's dangerous Forgotten Territories. But beneath the dry rivers and dead forests, a fiery myth is stirring from its sleep . . .

'. . . beautifully written.'
MALORIE BLACKMAN

'. . . an absolute jewel of a book . . . utterly magical.'
MELINDA SALISBURY

Paperback, ISBN 978-1-910002-74-2, £6.99 • ebook, ISBN 978-1-910655-58-0, £6.99

TRY ANOTHER GREAT BOOK FROM CHICKEN HOUSE

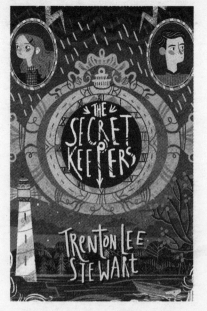

THE SECRET KEEPERS by TRENTON LEE STEWART

A magical watch. A string of secrets. A race against time.

When Reuben discovers an old pocket watch, he soon realizes it has a secret power: fifteen minutes of invisibility. At first he is thrilled with his new treasure, but as one secret leads to another, he finds himself on a dangerous adventure full of curious characters, treacherous traps and breathtaking escapes. Can Reuben outwit the sly villain called The Smoke and his devious defenders the Directions and save his city from a terrible fate?

'There are some genuinely haunting and ingenious moments as the three young heroes combat the villain in his mouldy mansion.'
THE NEW YORK TIMES

'. . . the tension never flags and the hold-your-breath moments come thick and fast.'
CAROUSEL

Paperback, ISBN 978-1-911077-28-2, £6.99 • ebook, ISBN 978-1-911077-29-9, £6.99